Special thanks

Allison Grier, Amber, Andrew Robinson, Anij Fallows, Anthony Kozak, Beth Barany, Bjorn Munson, Blaise Faint, Brendon Zee, Caelin Hill, Caledonia, Catherine Leja, Chad Bowden, Chris Call, Claire Ferguson-smith, CLTidball, Colleen Villasenor, Daniel Groves, Dave Baxter, Derek J. Bush, dhf, Dr. Charles Elbert Norton III, Edward Nycz Jr., Emerson Kasak, Eric Brooks, Erlinda Sustaita, Fred W Johnson, Gerald P. McDaniel, GMarkC, guardian J, Guillermo Sanchez, Heather Gearhart, Hollie Buchanan II, J. "Gwynn" Rentfleish, James Kralik. Janice Jurgens, Jared, Jeff Lewis, Jeffery Greathouse, Jennifer Johnson, Jennifer L. Pierce, Jeron Kuxhausen, John "AcesofDeath7" Mullens, John Albinsson, John Pankey, Jon, Jonathan Brown, Joshua Bowers, Joshua Chessman, Joshua Easter, Joshua McGinnis, KaS, Kelley RN, Kyle Rogers, Lisa Lyons, Lovelight Lioness Productions, Mark Newman, Mat Meillier, Matthew Johnson, Michael St. George Matatics, Michelle Marsh, Mike Connell, Monkey King Comics, Nari Muhammad, Nick Smith, Paul E. Olson, Paul Popernack, Paul Rose Jr., Paul Trinies, Paul Wocken, Philip Early, Robert Weimer, Scott Adams, Scott Kilburn, Sean Brislen, Sean Iffland, Shannon Carlin, Stabbath, Stephen, Taiga Char, Tom S, Victoria Nohelty, Vince, Vulpecula, Walter Weiss, and Weasel.

Also by Russell Nohelty

THE OBSIDIAN SPINDLE SAGA
The Sleeping Beauty
The Wicked Witch
The Fairy Queen
The Red Rider
THE GODVERSE CHRONICLES
And Death Followed Behind Her
And Doom Followed Behind Her
And Ruin Followed Behind Her
And Hell Followed Behind Her
And Conquest Followed Behind Them
And Darkness Followed Behind Her
And Chaos Followed Behind Them
Katrina Hates the Dead
Pixie Dust

OTHER NOVEL WORK
My Father Didn't Kill Himself
Sorry for Existing
Gumshoes: The Case of Madison's Father
The Invasion Saga
The Vessel
Worst Thing in the Universe
The Void Calls Us Home
The Marked Ones

OTHER ILLUSTRATED WORK
The Little Bird and the Little Worm
Ichabod Jones: Monster Hunter
Gherkin Boy
www.russellnohelty.com

The Dragon Champion

Book 2 of Dragon Strife

By:

Russell Nohelty

Edited by:

Lily Luchesi

Proofread by:

Katrina Roets

Cover by:

Paramita Bhattacharjee

Chapter 1

It wasn't easy to find peace after the incidents following my return to the village of Yesiburgh and the subsequent lynch mob that formed because of it. Even when we did find a form of peace, it was uneasy on the best days. There was a lot of bad blood between the town and the cedars after the incident on the volcano path, especially Renata. It took months for them to step foot into town, and even when they did, the citizens laid down snarls and catty snipes so thick, you could swim through them.

After so long in the caves, it wasn't easy for the cedars to integrate back into society, if they chose to do so at all. Those who lived in the volcano for decades had a wild, feral quality to them, and treated everything like a threat.

"And how did that make you feel, Nur?" I asked, seated around the circle of the group I set up for the cedars in the basement of the old church that rested on one end of the square where they used to celebrate our lives and toast to our deaths before the town sent us to our fate.

It took me weeks to walk through the grassy knoll where I spent so many afternoons in my youth, and even longer before my heart stopped beating like I was being chased by an angry bear. They really sent me to my death, and danced in the hours before it, like it was a cause for celebration.

"I don't like being called 'dragon meat'." Nur sighed. "I'm trying to run a legitimate business, and when they say things like that...well, I want to rip their faces off."

Nur was the first to move to town, after me, of course. The city council determined that all cedars could keep their homes as reparations for their trauma, but they would have to work to keep it.

That was easy for Nur. She knew how to cook, and the day she opened her bakery there was a line around the block for the sheer novelty of it. Leyhan's family didn't like the competition at first, but they swallowed their pride and helped anyway, and in time an equilibrium emerged that allowed both of their businesses to thrive.

Nur focused mostly on the essentials, hearty meat pies and thick baguettes so crusty it took both hands to snap in half. Leyhan's family specialized in more sweets and desserts, specialty items that Nur would have no reason to make during her time in the caves.

"Those people are just ignorant," Thorna growled. "They can pound sand for all I care."

Thorna hated that she had to work now but thought it a right bit better than being swallowed by a dragon or being forced to live in the caves with him after Dragon Lord Ewig spared her life.

"That's nice in theory," Mari said. "But it still hurts all the same. You don't know what it's like, coming back after being away, seeing people who thought you were dead…they still treat me like I'm dead sometimes. I hear my mother yelp sometimes when I come around a blind corner, like I'm a ghost."

"I'm sorry," Bella said. "That must suck."

Bella was going on six now, and Thorna just turned eleven. Life changed the least for them, especially Bella, because they hadn't been sacrificed yet. They were still in school and could be apprenticed easily enough. There was always room for small hands to do delicate work.

"It really does," Mari said, tears filling her eyes. "I feel like a burden half the time, and a freakshow the other."

Mari moved back home soon after Nur. The possibility for her own bedroom was too great. It wasn't until she returned to her old house that she realized they had given her room to her younger sibling. Families were supposed to keep the room pristine for visitors to worship at, but she had been gone a decade, and nobody bothered to visit her shrine anymore.

The townspeople had short memories, and that was the hardest part of us being around for them. We were a living memory of the horrors they allowed themselves to commit, and they didn't like the feelings that bubbled up inside themselves when they glanced at us. Once we were out of sight, we were out of their minds, and they could bury their guilt deep down. Now that we had returned to town, our presence ripped the scabs they tried so hard not to pick every time we walked down the street.

Still, I believed in the best in them; and that by being around, integrating into our little town of Yesiburgh, we could show people we were worth loving.

"That's horrible for both of you," I said. I didn't know how I became the de facto leader of the group, but the burden had fallen to me, like so many things. "And yet, you have not returned to the caves. Why?"

Fadia and Selma tried to live in town for a spell, but it was too much for them, so they retreated back to the safety and sanctity of the caves, and Renata, who never made her way to town.

"Why should I leave?" Nur said. "They are the ones who sent me to die. I didn't ask for that. This is my home just as much as theirs."

"That's a good point," I said. "This is our home just like theirs. In time, I think they'll realize that."

After the incident, the city council had a vote and agreed that only Renata would be held accountable for both the death of Mari's brother and the attempted murder of Leyhan. She would be arrested the minute she stepped back into town. The other cedars could integrate back into society as they pleased.

"And why should we be insulted in the meantime?" Bella spoke up.

However, Ewig made it clear that Renata was under his protection while she lived in the caves and would not be harmed without dire consequences for the town. They came to an understanding that Renata could come and go into town, as long as it was under Ewig's watchful protection, but that didn't stop her from staying away all the same.

"We shouldn't," I replied. "But there are more people who don't insult us than do. We have to remember that, even when it's hard." I turned to Mari. "And what about you? Have you thought about returning to the caves?"

"I...I thought about going back," she said. "But every time I do, I think about what Renata did to my brother." She started to cry again. "What I *let* her do to him, and I get violently ill. If I ever saw her again, I don't know how I could get by."

"You could leave," Thorna said. "To another town."

"And start over?" Mari's voice was meek as the tears ate at her words. "I thought about that, too. I even packed my bags one night, but..."

"But what?" I asked when her voice faded.

She shook her head. "I can't bring myself to do it. These people...they did horrible things to me...to all of us, but they are my family. There is history here. I'm not ready to wipe that all away and start again." She swallowed hard. "I still have those bags packed though, and one day, if I'm strong enough, I'll do it. I will."

I reached over and grabbed Mari's hand. "I, for one, hope you stay. I'll miss you like crazy if you go away."

"I'll miss you too, Gilda."

As we looked into each other's eyes, I saw a figure walk down the stairs into the basement. My eyes shifted focus to Sister Milka, who tapped her wrist and pointed to the clock on the wall, which had just turned over to noon.

"Is that the time already?" I asked.

"I'm afraid so," Sister Milka said, her lips pursed tightly. "We have church group starting soon."

I pulled my hand away from Mari and wiped the tears from the side of my eyes. "That was productive. I hope to see you all back here next week."

Chapter 2

Sister Milka was the hardest hit by the revelation that none of her precious cedars had been sacrificed. She dedicated half a century to our care and preparation to be the perfect gift for Ewig. The entire town believed the only thing standing between them and utter destruction was her guidance. She was given carte blanche to the resources of the town, and the townspeople lauded her with every step she took, because they thought she kept them safe. When that all fell apart with the revelation we were still alive, her standing in the community crumbled. She still had her devotees, but she no longer held even a fraction of the power she once did.

Now, the stern woman filled with confidence and bravado was gone, replaced with a meek, gray, hunched woman with no luster behind her eyes. If the town treated us with deference and revulsion at our existence, Sister Milka was treated with outright bitterness. She had been dragged in front of a tribunal after we returned to town. They accused her of being in concert with Ewig. They demanded an explanation for the great dragon's trickery, but she had nothing to offer except her truth.

Perhaps they saw how broken she was from the experience, or moved by how piteous she had become, because they let her go. The rest of the town would not be so kind. She was no longer invited to the grand parties at the elder estates, or to preside over prayers at holiday supper.

The church allowed her to remain in their service, in a reduced role, while they investigated the matter of our continued existence. She was not the prominent member of their community she once was though and had been relegated to church groups and school lessons.

I grabbed my bag slung over the chair and pulled a loaf of crusty rye bread from it, wrapped in a blanket.

"Here," I said as I handed it out to her. "Nur made this for you."

Her lips curled up in disgust. "I don't need your pity."

I leaned in closer to her. "We both know that's not true, but even if it were, this is not made from pity, but from love."

Her hand shook as she reached for the bread, and then darted forward to grab it from me hungrily. I could see in her eyes that she wanted to devour the bread all at once in front of her fledgling congregation, but her decorum took hold of her, and she simply stuffed it under her black dress.

"It's most appreciated."

"Do you need anything?" I asked.

I didn't know why I cared so much for Sister Milka. For over a decade she groomed me for death, and then when it was time, she led me to slaughter. Still, in that time, I had good days. I was well cared for, and even fawned over more often than not.

Besides, she was one of the few people who treated me like a human. Though the rest of the town refused to look me in the eye, she had no trouble with it. I might have only been a sacrifice to her, but at least she treated me like a human being, which was more than I could say about most of the town.

"Gilda." Nur touched my back. "I have to get back to the store. Are you coming?"

I nodded. "I'll be right there."

I said my goodbyes to Sister Milka as the cedars walked toward the stairs, walking by members of the church group as we passed. They looked upon us in horror, murmuring to themselves about how we besmirched the church's good name for sullying their precious basement with our existence.

I would not be beaten down by them. Instead, I raised my chin as high as I could, and pushed my shoulders back in false confidence. The best revenge was living and rubbing it in their faces how their church was a sham.

Most days I couldn't believe they still worshiped the dragon lords, especially when one of them had proven that their edict to sacrifice one girl every five years to secure their bounty was built upon a lie.

It was a comfortable lie, though.

That's what most people wanted. My mother used to tell me as much when I was young, but I never believed it. I thought given new information, people would open their eyes, and while some of them did, all too many shut them tighter, burrowing themselves in the blatant lies the church provided instead of confronting them.

"I don't know why you are nice to her," Mari said as we mounted the stairs toward the street. "She represents everything I hate about this place."

"She was a big part of my life for years. I love her still, even though I hate her. I can't just turn that off."

"You can surely try," Thorna said. She pushed an imaginary button on her chest. "See, it's off."

"I'm not sure it was ever turned on in your case," I replied, looking back to the church after we had exited onto the street. "She's still a human being. I see how people look at her, and how they look at us. I don't want to fight hate with hate. It's like fighting fire with fire. All you get is a bigger blaze."

"That's stupid," Bella said.

"Agreed," Thorna said, grabbing her hand. "I'll see you all next week, if not sooner. We have to get this one home, and I need to get ready for my apprenticeship tomorrow."

"Come hungry!" Nur said, smiling. "I'm making a thick stew for tomorrow, and you'll be my taster."

"Will do!" Thorna said, running off with Bella.

"Thank you for taking her," I said to Nur.

"When I heard nobody else would do it, what else could I do? She's a good kid."

"We were all good kids," Mari added.

"Yes, but they have the chance to remain good kids, instead of becoming broken women." Nur sighed. "I should get back. We'll be getting the dinner rush soon."

I kissed Nur on the cheek. "You sure you won't come tonight?"

"I left that life behind, but I made Ewig's favorite. Stop by in an hour and I'll have it ready for you by then."

"Will do," I said, watching her go off before turning to Mari. "Mom said she made too much food again, and you're welcome for dinner."

Mari laughed. "Doesn't she see me enough during the week?"

My mother reopened her tailor shop after I returned home. She worked out of the house and had enough business that she needed a second set of hands. Since nobody else wanted Mari, my mother took her in as an apprentice, though she was more skilled than even my mother already after years spent mending clothes, darning socks, and repurposing fabric as the cedar's seamstress.

"She loves you," I said. "And since I'm never home…"

I felt guilty about it, but it had been hard to look my mother in the eyes after what she did, and as happy as I was to see her when I returned home, the more days that went by, the more my joy was replaced by anger at her not stealing me away with my father, and for letting me walk to my death without even a plea for my life.

Luckily, there were plenty of things to keep me busy in town, especially now that I had been named to the city council to speak for the cedars, and Ewig.

"When are you leaving for the caves?" Mari asked.

"I have a council meeting, so after I do that and pick up dinner. Leyhan's supposed to meet me."

"I don't know how he can look Renata and the others in the eyes after what they tried to do to him."

"He's very good at turning the other cheek," I said with a smile. "That's   one of many things I love about him."

"Gross," Mari said. "Well, you have fun tonight. I'll tell your mother you said hi."

I waved her off as she disappeared into the street. She wouldn't admit it, but I knew she felt the same about her family as I did about my mother. It was hard to trust those that let you walk to your death. The dinners were awkward, and the conversations stilted, and home never felt safe. I doubted it ever would again.

I loved my mother, I did. But I hated what she did to me, and as much as I tried to turn the other cheek, I couldn't do it for her. Not yet, at least, and that broke my heart. Still, I would simply die if anything happened to her.

Chapter 3

Before the cedars returned, the town was run by three elders, but after we returned, the citizens demanded changes to how the city was run. Or at least some portion did. A large contingent of them still wanted to stick with tradition, and trusted the council's leadership, even after 100 years of sending our people to their "deaths" unnecessarily.

Luckily, enough of them were reasonable, and voted to dismantle the council of elders, and form a more progressive city council. The first council was comprised of Elderman Florence, from the previous council (the other two abstained from running), the ex-mayor, a local businessman, a well-off housewife, and myself, who was elected to speak for the cedars. Since there were only four of them in town, not including myself, I had the smallest voting bloc, which didn't win me any favors on the council, but every one of us had to contribute to the town running smoothly, and if my contribution was making sure no girls ever went to their deaths again, then that was a noble contribution to me.

"Good afternoon, Councilwoman Gilda," the ex-mayor said as he met me at the front of the gates. "Ready for today's meeting?"

I sighed. "Absolutely not, Councilman Edward. They are all so mercilessly tedious, aren't they?"

Councilman Edward laughed. "Wouldn't it be nice to be emperor, and be able to cut through the governmental red tape with a machete?"

I thought for a moment as we stepped into city hall. "No, I don't think it would. I think that would be quite a lonely existence."

"Then you are stuck with the way things are, I'm afraid."

I grumbled. "I don't much like that either."

City Hall had every government office contained inside of it, and even though it bustled with activity, it was quite a droll affair, with none of the flourishes of the school, or the garishness of the church. It was utilitarian, and nothing more.

"The wheels of democracy turn slowly," Councilman Edward said. "And it requires many tests of our sanity."

Councilman Edward turned right and opened a wood door. Inside sat the council chamber. Councilwoman Florence was already seated on the dais, behind the big wooden podium which raised us all up above the common rabble of the town.

Councilman Edward grabbed a cup of coffee and a bagel supplied by Nur's shop and took his place in the middle of the dais, as the highest chair. I did the same and took the seat at the far end, sitting lower than all the others, but still with a seat at the table.

Slowly, the room filled in with townspeople. Meetings were never well attended, and this one was no exception. We had little business of interest to the general public, but no matter the subject, some people always showed up to express their displeasure, and they were never, for lack of a better word, sane. It was a constant lesson in the saying "you can't please everyone."

Eventually, Councilwoman Theresa entered the room. She was a short, squat woman married to the town blacksmith. She wasn't expected to win, but in the end, she pulled off an upset by the slimmest of margins. Councilman Whitley was the final member of our entourage, and his opponent wasn't so lucky as to survive his onslaught of negative press they received from his paper.

"Can you please tell your friend Nur she makes the best bagels?" Councilwoman Theresa said, taking a bite. "I didn't even know you could put blueberries in them until I tasted hers."

"We had to cook with what we could find foraging the mountain," I replied. "She's very resourceful, but yes, I will tell her."

She took another bite. "You all have been such a boon to our little community. I'm so glad you're not dead." She stopped chewing and covered her mouth, horrified. "Oh, I'm so sorry, sugar. I didn't mean—I mean—"

I held up my hand. "It's okay, really. I'm glad I'm not dead, too."

Councilwoman Theresa was a kind woman and seemed to truly believe we were a net benefit to the town. She always met my eyes when we spoke and smiled sweetly when I spoke. There was none of the malice I saw from the rabble in front of me, who stared up from their sparsely populated wooden pews with malice in their eyes.

"Would you two biddies stop with the prattling?" Councilman Whitley growled. His suit was perfectly tailored, and his thick mustache was meticulously groomed. "We have work to do."

"I'm sorry, Councilman," I said with a smile. "I see your collar is a little bowed. My mother can fix that right up for you."

It wasn't, but it gave him such a fright that he rose from his seat to check himself in a pocket mirror he kept in his coat. When he realized I lied to him, he scoffed and blustered under his breath.

"Alright," Councilman Edward said, pounding his gavel. "Order, order. Let's get started."

There was little more than minutiae to go through during the meeting, which was usually the order of the day; whether we should use municipal funds to build a new light on Sycamore Street, a motion to declare one of the shops a historical monument, and another to tear said shop down to build a new bank. Both of them failed to be carried forward after little arguing between us, and even less conjecture from the gathered masses.

It wasn't until we opened up the floor for new business that a little, old woman stepped forward to a podium in the center of the room with a stack of papers. All eyes followed her toward the center of the room, and all the cross-chatter from the rabble died down.

"Thank you, council." She cleared her throat. "I bring forth a petition signed by over a hundred of your fellow townspeople demanding the cedars be formally reprimanded by the authorities of this town, forced to stand trial, and, when convicted, banished forever from the town we so love."

A huge round of applause boomed through the room. It was only then that I realized almost the entire gathered crowd had come to listen to the little, old lady beg the council, including myself, to kick me out of the only home I had known.

"Excuse me?" I said.

She turned to me and smiled sweetly. "It's no offense to you, dragon meat, but you are a blight to all of us, and your very existence could bring forth untold horrors on our small little town."

"And how would we do that?" I asked, angrily.

"Watch your tone," Councilman Edwards said to me. "I will also note you are speaking out of order. It is Councilwoman Theresa's time to speak first."

"I yield my time to her," Councilwoman Theresa said.

"As do I," Councilwoman Florence added.

"I don't need time yielded to me. I am the only cedar on this council, and I demand that this woman tell me how I could bring forth ruin on this town."

She never broke her smile when she talked. "It's very simple, dragon meat."

"Don't call me that!" I shouted.

"No need to get hostile." She smiled, and her crooked teeth shined for all to see. "The fact of the matter is simple. Rule of the land is that every five years, a young woman be sacrificed to the great lord of the territory. These are not our rules, they come from the emperor himself, and failure to do so could lead to the army razing our town and killing us all."

"But we were sacrificed!" I shouted.

"If that were true, then you would be dead." The old woman turned to the whole council. "By letting these women roam free, you are spitting in the face of the emperor himself and endangering every one of us. Do not let your guilt blind you to the truth. The lives of five women are not worth the destruction of our whole town."

"This matter has already been decided," Councilwoman Florence said. "When we ratified the new town charter, which was approved by a majority of your fellow villagers, we decided to absolve the cedars from any responsibility for Ewig's transgressions against the throne and give them safe harbor."

"That was because we all felt guilty for them, but now, in the sober light of day—" she shook the papers in her hand "—many of us have realized the truth and want to change our votes."

"You can't do that!" I shouted. "You already voted."

"Hush up, dragon meat!" she screamed. "You'll doom us all!"

"Your dissension is noted." Councilman Edward banged his gavel after scolding me again. "This is very distressing, but you make some claims that must be addressed, and the fact that you have over a hundred signatures means we must weigh what action to take."

"Are you kidding me?" I shouted. "This woman is a loon!"

"Watch your tongue," the woman said. "You do not speak for us, dragon meat. You speak for the very women who would be our blight."

The gavel slammed again. "Quiet, everyone. Now, I will ask for a vote on whether we should take up this matter." He held up his hand. "I vote aye."

"I second that motion," Councilman Whitley said.

"And I vote nay," I replied. "Wholeheartedly. We shouldn't even justify this with a vote."

"I second," Councilwoman Florence said. "This is preposterous. These women coming back to us is a miracle."

"It is a blight!" the woman screamed.

"Enough!" Councilman Edward boomed, before turning to Councilwoman Theresa. "And what say you?"

"This is very hard," the councilwoman said. "I do love their bagels, of course, and like you very much, Gilda, but this woman is from my district."

"And most of these signatures are from your district, by the way," the old woman said. "For the record."

"Please, Theresa," I said, turning up to her. "You know me. I'm not a blight. I'm not ruin. I'm not...dragon meat. I'm just a woman, like you, trying to make my way in the world."

She bit her lip. "I'm sorry, but this woman is a member of the community, too, which means her words have weight. I need time to review these signatures. If they are all valid and accounted for, then we have to take this seriously. So, I vote yay, the motion should proceed, for the time being."

The gavel slammed. "Motion carried. Please present your signatures for validation, and we will take up this matter in a month after further investigation."

"Thank you, councilwoman," the old woman said. "You just secured my vote for a second term."

She betrayed me. She looked me right in the face, after sitting next to me every day for months. She ate Nur's bagels, and still, she gave merit to these crazy people who think we should be banished. I wished I could be surprised, but nothing surprised me anymore.

How could somebody be so cruel?

Chapter 4

They voted to approve the motion. I thought that being on the city council would change things, but they still approved a motion to kick us out of our homes and treat us like pariahs. It was my worst fears realized.

No, it wasn't a binding resolution, and perhaps it was little more than a motion to look at the veracity of the claim, but it was such a ludicrous claim that it should have been summarily thrown out without note. Letting it fester gave those loons ammunition, and they could now chalk up a win to their crazy conspiracy against me and the other cedars. More importantly, giving them any fuel bolstered the idea that we were second class citizens, unworthy of the same rights as everyone else; that we weren't even worthy of being allowed to live.

"I'm sorry," Councilwoman Theresa said as she walked past me after the meeting. "It's just— you know how it is."

She wanted me to grant her clemency, but I had none for her. "Yes, I know how it is. I live with it every day. What I can't believe is that you would side with them."

"It's not that big a deal, Gilda," she scoffed. "We'll look through these signatures, call some witnesses, and it will show nothing, and then we can come back and tell them that we looked into it and decided not to move forward."

"That's not how this works. You give them an inch and they take a mile. Today they are asking you to review these signatures, but tomorrow they'll be asking for my head. That's how they work, eroding your will a little at a time. It's a dangerous game, Theresa, and I'm the pawn stuck in the middle."

I blew past her before she could say anything else. If I waited any longer to leave, she would have seen me cry, and more than anything I didn't want her to know how much she wounded me. When I pushed the door open outside, the old woman and her cronies were celebrating in the street like it was Ewig's birthday. When they saw me, they pointed and laughed.

"Do you see that, dragon meat?" the woman screeched. "Nobody wants you here, not even your precious city council members! Go away, dragon meat!"

Of course, they celebrated with frivolity because they thought they won. In that moment I wished I was emperor, so I could cut through the red tape and lop off their heads. Instead, I turned away from them as they hurled insults in my direction. I churned my legs faster and faster, until I broke into a sprint halfway across the square.

Maybe it would have been better if I died that day. If I was such a bother...if this was what I had to look forward to...if this was really what people thought of me, then why was I fighting for them to treat me like a human? No, Gilda. You can't fight hate with hate. Only love can do that.

Nur's bakery sat on the edge of the square, on a corner that took you down a side-street toward the edge of town, and my house. Nur sold most of her possessions to afford it, but it was hers, and she loved it. She hand-painted the sign on the front herself, and every morning wrote an inspirational slogan on the chalkboard next to the specials. Today's was "they can't keep you down forever."

Oh, how I wish I believed that one.

The smell of baked bread filled my nose as I strolled into the store to see her standing behind a small counter, counting money from her register. Behind her, the bread racks were almost empty.

"You're here!" Nur said with a smile, before seeing my forlorn face and her face dropped. "Woof, you look like you've gotten ten tons of bad news."

I couldn't help it. I fell into her arms and cried, and cried, and cried. Nur locked the door as a middle-aged man was trying to get in and pulled the curtains so I could have some privacy.

When I was finally done, she listened to what happened and shook her head. "Maybe we should just go. There has to be a place where we can start over."

"This is our home," I replied. "We deserve to be here just as much as them, and if they just tried...it would all be okay. I believe that."

"I know you do, but what good is people knowing who you are if you are thrown to the wolves? The best we can hope for is pity." She looked out the corner of the shade. "Pity brings in just as much money, so I'm not complaining, but I know why they keep coming. They think if they buy enough, they will remove their guilt, but it doesn't work that way. Guilt can't be bought off, only assuaged for a little while."

"Maybe they come because your stuff is delicious. It really is, too."

"Shut up, child. I know that, but that's not why they come. It might be why they come back, but I'm not even sure about that."

"Oh, by the way, Councilwoman Theresa told me to give you her compliments about the blueberries."

"Was this before or after she voted against us?"

"Before," I said. "On some level I don't even blame her. I only have five constituents, including myself. She's beholden to so many more people. Is it really her fault they hate us?"

"You trust in the good in people too much, Gilda. It's going to get you hurt one of these days." Nur nodded. "Yes. Her job is to represent people, but also to lead them. It's easy to be swept up in the chaos of the masses."

"If it's not her, they'll just elect somebody else, and they could be worse. Maybe they won't even like your bagels."

"Maybe, but what's the point of her liking my food if she doesn't see the whole of me? She's beholden to her people, but she still made the choice she did. When these people come for our heads, the blood will be on her hands, too."

I wiped my eyes. "I'm so sick of crying about this. I'm so sick of seeing the good in everyone, in forgiving everyone else, when they can't even treat me like a person."

Nur shrugged. "Unfortunately, it falls on the wronged to forgive more often than not."

I sighed. "Well, this is depressing. At least I'll have something to talk about tonight with the girls. It will certainly be a lively dinner. Do you have it ready?"

Nur nodded. "Of course. Let me get it for you."

Nur wrapped up a loaf of grain bread hot from the oven, and a big meat pie. She placed it into a thick hide container to scal in the warmth, and then handed it to me.

"There's plenty of innards in this pie. I know how much Ewig likes viscera."

"Oof," I said, my knees buckling. "I'm going to have Leyhan carry this one."

She tapped the top of the hide. "I need this back. It's my best platter."

"I'll bring it back tomorrow."

"That'll do." She smiled. "Tell them hello for me, and that I love them."

"I will."

"It's going to be okay," Nur said, returning behind the counter.

"I know."

"I was saying it more for me than for you. Honestly, I'm not sure I believe it."

"Then I'll believe it for you, and you believe it for me, okay?"

She knocked lightly on the counter of her store. "I think I can do that."

"Me too, and if not, all we can do is try."

Chapter 5

I walked awkwardly through the town with the platter and bread stuffed in my arms. Before I was sacrificed to Lord Ewig, the townspeople looked away from me, trying their best to avert their eyes to assuage the guilt growing in their bellies at the sight of me. Now, they wouldn't even look at me, and when they did, it was all too often with malice.

I never thought I would miss the guilt in people's eyes, but this was worse. Either way, it was denying my humanity and replacing it with their ideal of what I should be, but I very much disliked being hated, even more than being pitied.

I shifted my weight to my right hip, and doing so dislodged the platter from my hands, and it tumbled to the murky ground below. I turned to grab it before it touched the ground but caught the bottom of my dress with my foot and tripped over it, falling to my hands and knees.

"Are you okay?" I heard somebody say as they rushed toward me. I looked up to see a red-headed girl with freckles speckling her fair skin. While the others turned from me as if I didn't exist, or chuckled under their breath at my plight, she dropped down to her knees and lifted me up before returning to the ground to pick up the platter.

"I think I'm fine, Bernice. Thank you."

She brushed the dirt off the hide that covered the platter. "Luckily, it landed right side up. I don't think anything spilled out or anything."

"Thank the gods for that," I replied. "I'll take it."

She pulled the bowl close to her. "You look a fright. Why don't I hold this while you clean yourself up?"

I walked over to a window where I could see myself in the reflection. She was right. My hair was a mess, and dirt covered the bottom of my face, along with my hands and knees.

"Here." Bernice pulled a handkerchief out of her dress and handed it to me. "It's not much, but it'll help."

I smiled as I grabbed the handkerchief and wiped the dirt off my face. "That's very kind of you."

"Mama always told me that kindliness was next to godliness. Of course, it's not polite to talk about the gods these days."

She was right. Since the dragons banished the gods from our planet, it had been forbidden to speak of them, even the cliches and parlances that had no religious bent to them.

"Your mother is a brave woman saying things like that." I brushed the dirt from my hands with the handkerchief, and then finished off what was left on my dress once the cloth got too dirty. "That sort of thing will get you arrested."

She smiled at me. "I'm not scared of anybody. I'm talking to you, after all, aren't I?"

I nodded at her and turned from the window. "You are at that, which might be the most dangerous thing of all." I beckoned her forward. "Let me take that from you and get out of your hair before people start to talk."

Again, she pulled the platter away from me. "Where are you headed? I could carry this for you a ways."

"Off to the edge of town. I'm meeting my boyfriend."

"That Leyhan fella, right?" she asked. "I like him. Is he gonna be angry you went to another baker for your dinner?"

I laughed. "I don't think so. Less work for him to do, after all." I took a deep breath, my eyes narrowing at her. "You really don't mind being seen with me, do you?"

She shook her head. "Not at all. People can't take much more from me at this point."

"Very well then." I turned to the road. "If you can carry that for me, it would be most appreciated."

My right ankle was sore as I put weight on it, but I tried to hide it the best I could. Any sign of weakness could send the vultures to pick over my carcass. Still, it was impossible to hide the limp when I put weight on it.

"You need a doctor to look at that?" Bernice asked.

I squeezed the bread in my hand to fight the pain. "I don't think so. Just rolled it funny. I'll be fine."

"Headed up to the volcano?" She wasn't sheepish with her words. Most people in town didn't much like thinking about Ewig, or the women that kept time with him.

"Yes. I'm meeting some friends for dinner." I cocked my head to her. "What's it to you?"

She shrugged. "Just trying to make conversation. I always loved dragons since I was a kid, even though they ate people. When I found out Ewig hadn't eaten any of you, I got even more interested in him. Did you know he landed the fatal blow on Unestra that sent the other gods scattering?"

I shook my head. "He never said anything about that."

"Oh," she said. "Well, that's what I read in the history books, anyway. I have so many questions for him. You think maybe—you think I might join you one day?"

I stopped. "You want to come with me to the mountain?"

"Yeah, why not?"

It shouldn't have been surprising, but nobody, not even my mother, ever asked to go to the volcano with me.

"It's just—how old are you?"

Her face beamed with a bright smile. "Sixteen, just like you. Old enough to be sacrificed, so old enough to meet a dragon, I figure."

We crossed the main street and down an alley, at the end of which was the path to the mountain.

"Ewig is pretty secretive, and he doesn't like visitors much, but let me talk to him and see what he says."

Her eyes went wide. "Wow, that would be great. I won't be a bother, I promise. It's just, I am completely fascinated by him, and you." When I looked over at her, she darted her eyes away. "Sorry. I don't wanna be forward or anything, and not in a weird way. It's just that not many people have ever survived a dragon encounter, and you're one of them."

"It's nice to see somebody has nice things to say about us."

"There are plenty of others like me. We just stay in the shadows usually. The ones that hate you...they aren't all of us. I wanted you to know that."

We reached the end of the road, and Leyhan turned to me with a bright, chipper smile. He grew even more strapping with every day as he aged into his body, and it filled out with muscles borne from working the fires in the kitchen all day.

"Come take this from Bernice," I said, beckoning him over.

"Hello to you, too," he said, rushing over and kissing me on the cheek before grabbing the platter from Bernice. "This is a heavy one."

"Yes, I'm aware," I replied. "That's why I'm so appreciative of Bernice's helpfulness." I turned to her. "Thank you, seriously, for showing me there is still kindness in this town."

"There really is," Bernice replied, bowing slightly. "We're all rooting for you."

I mustered a smile for her. "Are you willing to do something else for me, then?"

She nodded. "Anything in my power."

"Bring as many people as you can gather to the next council meeting. Show my colleagues that not everyone hates my sisters."

She scratched her neck. "I'll sure try, Gilda, but like I said, we don't like to make ourselves known as sympathizers. The others, they are nasty folks, as you know."

"I know." I stepped toward her. "And that is why I need you to be brave, okay? If good people don't step up, I fear what will happen to us."

She swallowed hard. "I'll do the best I can, ma'am. You have my word."

"Thank you."

Chapter 6

It wasn't a short trip around the mountain to the back entrance of the volcano, but the short way up was an unstable and unsteady path that plummeted precariously into a thousand-foot drop. It was quite easy to lose your footing and plunge to your death. It amazed me that Sister Milka forced the girls to walk such a treacherous path, but then again, the forest beyond the volcano was forbidden, so how would she have known a simple path existed behind it?

"Do you want me to punch her?" Leyhan asked after I finished telling him what happened at the city council meeting and the old woman who assaulted me with her gang of cronies.

We had been walking for a long time, and I deferred talking about it for a long time, preferring idle chit chat and the silence of the forest, but eventually I felt comfortable enough to tell him the truth.

"Kind of, but then you would have to punch half the town."

"Maybe we can convince one half of the town to punch the other half."

"Oh, we could," I said. "But it would be the wrong half. The half that hates me are belligerent bullies, and they scare everyone else. That poor girl, Bernice, I don't know if she realizes how much she endangered herself helping me today."

"She knew," he replied. "She comes into the bakery quite a bit, and she always talks highly of you. Trust me, she knows what she's doing."

"I don't want her to get hurt. I don't want anyone to get hurt because of me."

Leyhan brushed past a low-hanging branch, and then held it up for me to walk under. "It's not right, the way some of the townspeople are treating you. People are starting to see that, or maybe they have always seen it, and now they are getting sick of it."

"It sure doesn't feel that way. It feels like fewer people are on our side every day."

"That's because the jerks are emboldened by things like Councilwoman Theresa buckling under their pressure. You said there were a hundred signatures on that sheet, right?"

"I don't know the exact number, but they said over a hundred."

"Well, if it was much more than that, they would have said a higher number. Do you know how many people live in Yesiburgh?"

"They haven't had a census in a long time, but—"

"Close to two thousand," Leyhan interrupted. "A hundred's not a lot of signatures, in the end."

"That's just the people who are willing to put their name to paper, Leyhan," I said. "What about all the people who feel that way and don't want to say it out loud?"

"Listen, I've seen those jerks around, trying to drum up signatures for their bitterness. They stopped in front of my store a couple times, and I had to shoo them away. I can tell you for a fact that most people looked at them like they were crazy."

I sighed. "I hear what you're saying, but it doesn't feel that way to me."

"Then maybe you should get your own petition going. See how many people really do support you and are willing to put their name to paper. I'll bet it's a fair bit more than a hundred."

"It's an interesting thought." I bit my lip. "But I don't want people to do it out of pity."

"Who cares why they want you to stay?" Leyhan gripped the platter tighter. "You are very frustrating. You are quick to latch on to anybody saying anything negative about you, but you can't even fathom the possibility that people support you, despite overwhelming evidence."

"What evidence?" I said.

"Hello!" Leyhan waved one of his arms in the air. "How about me, walking with you, to dinner with the people who tried to kill me, and the dragon who almost burned down our town because of it."

"That's different. We're in lo—" I stopped myself. Even though he said it to me often, I still had trouble admitting that I loved Leyhan to myself. "We're dating."

I didn't know why I held back saying it, like there were only a finite number of times I could tell him before the spell I used to entrap him wore off, which made the word lodge on my throat every time I went to say it.

"I don't come to your church group, or any of the other things you do. We are dating, but I'm not your lapdog. I have every right to stay away from these people, and yet I come anyway, because I believe in establishing and keeping good relations with Ewig, Renata, Selma, and Fadia. Bernice believes in that, too. I can see it in her eyes and feel the passion when she comes into the shop to talk about it."

"I don't..." I couldn't finish my sentence. All I could do was look down at the ground.

He lifted my chin up with the knuckle of his index finger. "And she's not the only one, by the way. People know we are dating, and they come in to show their support all the time. They patronize Nur's bakery, and buy clothes from your mother, because they want to support you."

"Because they pity us."

"Some of them, maybe, but not all of them. Some of them believe in you." Leyhan brushed past the woods into a clearing beyond. "Come to work with me tomorrow, and I'll show you. You can stay in the back, hidden, and just listen to people talk about you cedars. It's really something."

I nodded. "Okay."

As I moved into the clearing with Leyhan, I saw Fadia's farm stretched out in front of us. Now that she didn't have to hide herself on the mountain, she expanded through the clearing, growing all sorts of plants, and foraging fruit from the forest. She supplied several shops, including both Leyhan and Nur's, with produce and grain.

As we walked forward, Fadia dropped her hoe and waved at us. "About time you showed up. We were wondering if you forgot about us."

The sun was cresting over the horizon. "I'm sorry. I always forget how long the walk takes, and well...I will tell you all together."

Her face dropped. "I don't like the tone of your voice or look on your face."

"That's a good instinct."

Chapter 7

Fadia's farm rested near the base of the path that led up into the caves, but it was an hour climb to its mouth. We passed the small crack I shuffled out of when I saved Leyhan, what felt like an eternity, but was merely a year ago.

Things were so much easier back then. I had a path and knew my destiny. It was a horrible fate, but how many people could say with certainty they knew their purpose in life? A handful at most. I had been pointed in a singular direction my whole life, and, on some level, I missed it.

Not the death, of course. That would have been awful, but the world pointed me forward with clarity, with a certain fate at the end of it. Now, I was awash with choices, and nothing was certain. All I could do was follow my own moral compass, but what if that compass didn't point true north? No matter what I did, though, I couldn't shake the feeling that it was leading me askew.

I never had the knots in my stomach that filled my waking days, or the feeling of uncertainty that bubbled through my whole body every minute of every day, before I returned to town after the cedar, and now every move I made filled me with more questions than answers.

Was allowing Bernice to help me a positive or negative? Should I have been stronger at the meeting this afternoon? Was there something I could have said to prevent Theresa from voting for that awful bill, and seeing reason? Was I even the right choice to join the city council? Would Mari have been a better choice, or maybe Nur? The council certainly feared my cedar sisters more than me, and probably would have listened harder when they spoke.

It felt like every word I said rolled off the back of everyone but Councilwoman Florence. She was the only one who was consistently on my side, and then only because she saw the friend she lost to the great dragon lord. She asked me after I returned to the village if Ewig killed her Petunia, and there was great relief when she found out that he didn't, but she still lost her all the same.

I told her how her friend died on the mountain after a good, long life and was buried at the caldera. All the years she lived so close to Petunia, and yet they lived such different lives. If only they knew the truth sooner, perhaps they could have found each other again. That guilt was the only thing that kept Councilwoman Florence on my side.

"You have been quiet for a long time," Fadia said as we passed her old farm. "It's unlike you."

"I'm usually quiet," I replied, quite nearly offended.

"Not this quiet," Fadia said, brushing some dirt off her hands. "Whatever you have to tell us must be very important. Can you really not give me a sneak peek?"

"I could," I replied. "But I won't, because I know you can't keep a secret. I need everyone to hear this from me at the same time."

She held up her hands. "Fine, fine. Be that way."

Fadia was quiet for the rest of the trip up the mountain, which wasn't easy for her. She was a complete chatterbox, but the only one she had to speak with was Leyhan, and she still hadn't come to terms with what she had done to him.

Eventually, we reached the cave entrance. It was much like I remembered, with a long table in the center, and a hearth on the left side, where Nur had made all the meals. Now, Selma stood over it, watching the bubbling cauldron.

"They're here," Fadia said.

"And we brought meat pie," Leyhan said.

"It's really more of a cobbler now since it kind of fell," I corrected. "And some bread."

"Well bring it over here, then," Selma said. "And give me a hug."

We embraced for a long moment while Leyhan left the meat pie on a long cooking table they procured from town. Mari had four strapping men bring it up for them, probably to assuage her guilt for leaving them, especially Selma. For a long time, they were thick as thieves, and her leaving caused a rift between them.

"Where's Renata?" I asked, placing the bread on the table. "And can I heat this pie up somewhere?"

She nodded. "Just put it over the steam and it will come to a boil soon enough."

I did as she asked and then walked to the cooking table, where I picked up a knife and began to cut the exceptionally crusty bread.

"As for your other question," Fadia said, "she's up at the caldera."

"Again?" I said. "I already told her Leyhan has forgiven her."

"I wouldn't go that far," he replied, from the table after pouring himself a glass of wine. They had it delivered by the case, often in barter for food from Fadia's garden, or hides from the animals Renata trapped. "But she doesn't have to hide from me."

Selma laughed. "That's funny, since she's hiding because she thinks you're scared of her."

He sighed. "I'm—not—alright, that is fair. I am completely petrified of that woman, but I've eaten with her before, and it's fine."

"I'm going to get her." I walked toward the edge of the cave. "Play nice, okay?"

"I will if they will," Leyhan said.

Chapter 8

There were far fewer beds in the cave above the dining area than there were a year ago. Now that there would never be more girls coming to stay with Ewig, the cave had been converted to three larger spaces, with the twin beds now pushed together to make larger beds, along with dressers and changing areas for each of them. While they did not live in town, that did not mean they didn't pick up pieces from there, or patronize Mari's tailoring to get fabulous new clothes, especially Selma.

The only one who did not venture into town ever was Renata, forcing the others to take her kills for sale at the market. The deal the council struck with Ewig was that as long as Renata lived in the mountain, she could not be touched. It didn't mean she couldn't come to town to barter, but she still didn't. "Why go where I'm not welcome?" she always said.

She was always the feral one, even when I first met her. Fadia and Selma were homebodies, er, cavebodies, but Renata preferred to be lost in the forest for days on end. Often when I came for dinner she was gone on a hunt, only to come back days later with the skin of a bear and enough deer meat for months.

They still jerked and canned their own food, but now they were able to get more variety in town when the need, or desire, arose. I still would have appreciated them to live in town so people could see we weren't wild, vicious things, but that was a battle I fought and lost too many times for comfort.

I continued up the hill to the hot springs that bubbled in the cavern above the bedrooms. I stepped through the hot mugginess and found the crack in the back of the room which led to the caldera. There was a small footpath that took you around to the top of the volcano as well, but it was far more treacherous.

At the top of the volcano the heat mixed with the cool of the night air. I looked down for a minute into the molten lava that oozed below me. If it ever bubbled over, the town would be destroyed in hours. The main reason we had sacrificed girls to Ewig for a century was for his protection against that horrible fate.

I followed the caldera around to the other side, where I found Renata dangling her feet over the edge, looking at the hazy town below.

"You're getting predictable," I said.

"There's nothing wrong with being consistent," she replied, turning to me. "It means I'm stable."

"Stable is not a word I would use to describe you."

She chuckled. "I'm surprised to see you."

"I literally come every week."

"And every week I'm surprised to see you."

I walked forward and dropped down to sit with her. Under us, Yesiburgh sprawled out, until the forest collapsed around it and extended into the distance, with little pockets of clearing between the canopies. "You're my constituents. I have to see how you're doing, since you won't voluntarily come into town."

"Why would I want to go to a town that wants to kill me?"

"To see your friends," I replied.

"That's cute." She scoffed at me. "I don't have friends down there. Friends don't abandon each other."

"It's not abandoning, Renata. We wanted more than the caves could offer. What were we supposed to do?"

"Stay here where it's safe? Besides, we both know I would be arrested if I stepped foot into town."

"Not unless you leave Ewig's care. As long as you live here, they can't touch you—they won't touch you. You could still visit but..." I sighed and took a deep breath. She had a way of riling me up. "I don't want to fight with you."

"We're not fighting. We're arguing. There's a difference."

"I don't want to argue with you, either."

"That seems to be all we know how to do."

"It doesn't have to be like that. I care about you. We're friends, whether you like it or not."

"That's not how friendship works."

I nodded. "It's how this friendship works. You're one of 20 people in the whole world that knows what it's like to be sacrificed to a dragon."

"Not true. There are 11 other dragons. So, we're really one of like 200."

"I'm assuming those dragons ate their prey, and we're the only ones left."

"I don't know why you would assume that. We only know one dragon, and he let his cedars go. Why would the others be any different? It's quite possible it's all an act."

"I think that's hopeful thinking. I don't think it's helpful."

"That's funny, you are lecturing me on hopeful thinking, when literally every word out of your mouth is the same hopeful nonsense."

I shrugged. "You're right, but I still think you should think about moving down to town. We could use you down there."

"And I think you all should move back up here, where it's safe, and where people actually want you around."

There was a long silence as we stared at each other, both of us hoping the other would break. It was a fight we had a hundred times before, and neither of us had the emotion to carry it on like we once did. At the beginning, we nearly came to blows over it, but now, we were like two fighters circling each other after a long bout, exhausted and stumbling over each other.

"Nur made rabbit pie."

"Good. I'm glad my kills went to a good home."

I rose to my feet. "I think we should go eat it now and forget all this unpleasantness."

"Sweep it under the rug, like we always do." She eyed me. "Eventually, it's going to come to a head, and you'll wish you listened to me."

"Maybe, but not today." I held out my hand. "Are you coming?"

She turned from me. "I'll be along in a minute."

Chapter 9

There was a time when I looked up to Renata. I thought she was the strongest person I knew, but the truth was closer to the opposite. Hiding yourself on a mountain and stealing yourself behind a dragon wasn't brave, it was about the weakest thing you could do.

Real strength came from standing in front of your fears and moving forward anyway. It was owning a bakery in the center of town, and opening up to the public, despite the fact that some of those very members of the public wanted to kill you, or at least exile you from their sight. Real strength came from fighting for people who weren't like you, just because it was the right thing to do.

Renata might have been physically strong, but she was weak where it mattered—where we needed her to be strong; where we needed her to lead, she cowered from it.

By the time I reached the dining cavern, I still wasn't over my conversation with Renata. The others must have seen the scowl on my face because they didn't attempt to let me into the easy, lazy conversation they were having at the table over a bottle of wine.

"Pie's piping hot," Selma said.

I grabbed a big knife and cut a heaping portion, careful to add as many entrails as I could to the bowl before I placed the knife back on the edge of the cooking table.

"I'm bringing this to Ewig."

Nobody objected. By now my routine was known by all. First, I tried to coax down Renata for a spell, and then I brought Ewig dinner. Afterwards, I came back for dinner, where Renata would make an appearance before disappearing once her plate was cleared.

I made my way carefully up the stairs and over the rope bridge that had been reinforced with heavy rope over the past year. The path to Ewig's clearing was still dark, with only a small light flickering at the end from the fire that he always had burning.

"You're late," the great red dragon growled when I entered the cave clearing. He pushed his paws into the ground and lifted himself up, stretching first forward and then back, before rolling his shoulders and giving a big yawn up to the Heavens.

"City council meeting ran long." I held up the bowl for him. "But I brought this from Nur. She sends her best."

"Hrm," Ewig replied. "Not best enough to show up herself, though."

I placed the pie down for him. "You know how hard it was for her to leave. Mari too."

Ewig took a bite of the pie. "I don't begrudge them their independence. I just thought they would come back at least once. They didn't even come celebrate my birthday with me."

"They celebrated in town with the rest of Yesiburgh," I replied.

"You came," he said, taking more of the stew. "You even wore a silly, little hat."

"Everyone is different," I replied. "I process this whole thing by coming to see you, and they do it by staying away, just like Renata. You don't have to like it to respect it."

"I know you are right, but it doesn't hurt any less."

"I'm going to keep trying to get them to come, and maybe one day they will. Hopefully while they still have a choice."

Ewig's ears perked up. "What does that mean?"

"Nothing, it's just... People are not being very nice right now, and it's a slap in the face. I'm really trying, but it feels like everything is breaking down around me."

"Do I need to burninate some people?" Ewig said. "I could do it, you know."

I chuckled. "That's very sweet, but I— speaking of, I heard something today. I met a girl who said you laid the final blow on Unestra that ended the war. Is that true? I didn't learn that in school."

He sighed. "You know I don't like talking about this kind of thing."

"I know, but a friend brought it up today, and it had me wondering. I'd always read Ramidion landed the final blow to end the war."

He nodded. "Yes, that is what she wants you to think. Lord forbid anyone think a weak, small thing like me could do something so great as end a war."

"It's true then?"

"In its way. It is true that I landed the final blow, but my sisters and brothers weakened the goddess to a point where I could end her."

"That's amazing! Why don't you tell people the truth and set the record straight?"

"Because it is not something I am proud of. I dislike killing, and even more so with each passing day. Why would I want to glorify my brutality? All I want is peace."

"I'm sorry—you're right. I'm sorry."

"It's not your fault," he said, before curling himself up. "I am just cranky and tired."

"Of course," I said, backing away. "You know, my friend also asked if she could come up here and meet you. It would mean the world to her."

"I don't do visitors. I am not some sort of freakshow."

"It's not like that. Lots of people, they're in awe of you."

"That's even worse. I refuse to hold court like my brothers and sisters. If they are in awe of me, they can be in awe from a distance."

I nodded. "I told her I would try, and I did. I'll let her know what you said."

"Good," he growled, wrapping himself up in a tight, cozy circle. "Tell Nur thank you for the pie. It was delightful, but please, more innards next time."

"I will let her know. Goodnight, Ewig."

Chapter 10

"I don't know why you're surprised," Renata said after I told her, and the other cedars, everything that happened at the City Council meeting. "Of course they hate us. We are a reminder of their flawed logic. They will do anything to get rid of that reminder, which is why you should move back here."

"We're not going to change any minds by staying locked in this volcano," I replied.

"Who cares about changing minds?" Fadia chimed in. "This is about survival, and if they don't want us, then we don't want them, either."

"How can you say that, Fadia? You trade with these people." I looked over at Selma. "You use their furniture." My eyes tilted up to Renata. "You sell them your furs."

"We got along just fine without them for years," Selma said. "We can do it again. I'm with Renata. This is why I didn't want to move down to town in the first place. I don't go where I'm not wanted."

"We can fix this," I said. "You just have to come down to town and help us. When it's just the three of us, we can only do so much."

"Do you think that will really help?" Renata asked.

"I do—"

"Because I don't," she continued, cutting me off. "Having more memories of their heartlessness is going to make them even madder. You would do well to come up here and let them have their silly delusions."

I kicked off from the table. "I can't do that. I can't let them believe their stupid little lies. I can't let them forget that they sent us to our deaths."

"Then you will keep aggravating a raw nerve," Fadia said. "And eventually their anger will boil over."

"I don't believe that," Leyhan shot up to defend me. "You all tried to kill me, and I got over it. They can too."

"Poor, sweet Leyhan," Selma said. "You are more forgiving than most...than almost anyone, honestly. You're definitely more forgiving than me. They literally tried to kill us, and most of them can't forgive that we had the audacity to live. I tried to forgive them, to live with them, once. Never again. They hate us and that will never change."

"The loud ones, maybe," Leyhan said in reply. "But I think there are more people like me than there are like them."

"Then you are naïve," Renata growled.

She was so stubborn and maybe she was right. If she was going to be like this, we didn't need her type of help, but I thought maybe Selma would at least see reason.

"Divided, we will never succeed." I sighed. "Is that what you want?"

"Don't bring this on us," Renata replied. "I refuse to justify my existence or fit into their worldview that we are the villains in this story."

"Will you at least speak to them, if we can arrange it?" I looked at Fadia and then Selma, who turned their eyes to Renata. "Please."

She thought for a moment. "If they want to come break bread with us here, in our space, then I will hear them out, but I don't believe they have anything worthwhile to say."

"Maybe not, but if they can at least see you are human: a real, flesh human, and not some construction of their mind, maybe they will change."

"They saw us as human for fifteen years," Fadia said. "Each of us, and you. Yet they still sent us to our deaths. Anyone who can do that, I don't much care what they have to say."

"Will you come to dinner if I bring them here?" I asked.

Fadia nodded. "I will listen politely, but if they try to invalidate my existence, the conversation will cease."

"Fair enough," I said, eyes moving to Selma. "And you?"

"I don't really care what they have to say, but if they bring the food so I don't have to cook and clean up, then I'll eat with them."

I smiled. "I'll try to bring Mari, too."

Selma's cheeks flushed. "I'm—I don't care—but okay."

"There you have it then," Renata said. "That is as reasonable as we have any reason to be—more so, actually. They should be coming on their hands and knees, begging for an apology."

"I think that's asking too much," I replied.

"That's another place where you and I differ then," Renata said. "Because I think that's the least they can do for sending us to our deaths. Instead, all I ask is that they don't insult us in our own house."

"I will see what I can do."

"Or don't," Selma said. "We really don't care. We got along just fine before this, and we can get along just fine without them, too."

As I broke away to start cleaning the dishes, a bright flash of light shot down the cave, erupting from the tunnel that led to Ewig's room. My eyes went wide as I looked over to Renata, who was already rushing to the stairs.

I followed behind her, with the others behind me. The bridge swayed considerably as we ran across it, aggravating my sore ankle. I tripped and tumbled as I rocked from one side to the other, before making it to the other side. I looked back at the others, but Renata was already halfway down the tunnel, so I had no choice but to follow her.

"You dare enter my cave without permission!" Ewig's voice boomed through the tunnel.

Fire shot through the cavern from Ewig's nostrils as we entered the opening, lighting the room with a brilliant orange glow. Beneath him, a tiny man in a set of chain mail armor, his tunic emblazoned with the red and gold seal of the capital, a serpent dragon coiled around a tower.

"I don't mean to be a bother," the man chittered out as his whole body quivered. "Or cause offense."

"You dare enter this place wearing my sister's colors and claim not to cause offense!"

"Ewig!" I shouted, walking forward. "Please, calm down."

"You don't understand—" Ewig let out a deep growl before his anger dissipated. "This is a herald from the capital. I have not seen one in many ages. His appearance could be nothing but trouble."

I held up my hands to him. "If it is, he is just the messenger." I turned to him. "Isn't that right, sir?"

He nodded. "Nothing so formal, ma'am. I'm no knight. I do come with a message from Lord Bessinger, your grace."

Even at the edge of the world we had heard of Lord Bessinger, captain of the Emperor's army. His grandfather fought with the dragons in their war against the gods, and his father was the captain of the King's guard, before the king became the emperor with the merging of the dragon and human powers together under one common rule.

"And what does Lord Bessinger say?" I said. Behind me, everyone had caught up to us, and were sucking wind at the entrance to the cave, save for Renata, who's eyes shot daggers at the messenger. "Go on. We will not shoot the messenger, or burn them, as the case may be. Isn't that right, Ewig?"

He grumbled. "I suppose so."

The herald eased his grip on a scroll in his hand. He pulled a small dagger out of his belt and cut the wax seal, before unfurling it.

"His greatness," the herald said. "Lord Bessinger will arrive on the morn, to deal with the problem of the cedars who were intended as sacrifice to Dragon Lord Ewig, but were allowed to live, in violation of the Black Charter. For the good of the kingdom, Lord Bessinger will speak for the Emperor on this, and all matters. Signed, Emperor Paraphal III."

When he was finished, all I could think was one thing: perhaps Ewig should have burnt him to a crisp, because that was the worst news I had ever heard.

Chapter 11

"Gimme that!" Renata shouted, stomping forward and ripping the scroll from the herald's hand. She read the whole scroll, word by word, before her face dropped. "Well, poop."

"What does he mean, 'deal with the problem'?" Fadia said.

"Why are they sending the commander of the royal guard?" Selma added. "Have you heard the stories of Lord Bessinger's brutality? He will slaughter whole villages to prove a point."

"It's going to be okay," I said, walking forward with an unearned smile.

"It's not going to be okay!" Renata shouted, crumpling the scroll in her hand and throwing it into the fire. "This is what I have been saying this whole time. We're a blight on the whole empire. They won't stop until we are dead."

"We aren't going to let that happen," Leyhan said, stepping forward. "We're not going to let them take you all from us."

"We're not yours to give!" Selma shouted. "You lost that privilege when you sent us to our deaths."

"Hey!" I shouted. "Leyhan wasn't alive when you were sacrificed, Selma, or you, either, Fadia, so cut him some slack."

"He was alive when I was sacrificed," Renata said. "And did nothing to stop it."

"And I'm sorry about that," Leyhan said. "I did nothing to stop you from being sacrificed, and you tried to kill me. I thought that might make us even."

It was the logic that the city council used to avoid arresting any of the cedars for their part in Mari's brother's death, and Renata's attempted murder of Leyhan. It didn't make an ounce of logical sense, but the more I learned about the council, the less sense it made.

"No," Renata said. "It just makes us all bad people."

"Enough," I said, moving between them. "Can we decide what we're going to do about this before we have an army invading our town?"

"We aren't going to let you be taken," Ewig said, assuredly. "That much is certain."

"I think we need to get Mari and Nur here, so we can create a united front."

"I agree," Ewig said.

"And I'll try to rally as many people as possible to our cause," Leyhan said. "I know some of the more ardent supporters of you ladies, and hopefully we can create a chain of people, each informing the others."

"That sounds like a pretty good plan," Fadia said.

"Don't get it twisted," Renata growled. "Our detractors will learn of this soon enough, and they will come out en masse as well."

"Then it's time to test my theory that there are more of us than there are of them," Leyhan said. "I guess by tomorrow we'll see which of us is right."

"I hope for all our sake it's you," Selma said. "The emperor does not take kindly to towns that stand up to him."

"Will you come to town with me?" I asked the cedars. "I need to get Mari, Nur, and my mother, and get back here before sunrise."

"I'm not going anywhere," Renata said.

"This is Nur and Mari we're talking about," Leyhan said.

"And they made their choice."

Fadia sighed. "I'll come with you."

"You're making a mistake," Renata said.

"And it's mine to make." She turned to Selma. "How about you? I know you're mad at Mari, but I can't imagine you want to put her in danger."

Selma kicked the dirt in the room. "Fine. I'll come. I won't like it, but I'll come."

"That's good enough for me."

"Meanwhile," Ewig said, "I will work on fortifying the volcano so that none can come up the path behind us, forcing them to traverse the narrow, dangerous route in front of us."

"That sounds like as good a plan as any," I said. "What do we do about the herald?"

Ewig smiled. "Return to your camp, and tell your master that we will see him, alone, tomorrow, when he arrives. If his people hurt anyone in this town, especially my girls, I will see personally to it that he burns where he stands."

The herald quaked in his boots but summoned his strength enough to nod. "Yes, Your Majesty."

He turned and rushed out of the cave. When he was gone, Leyhan and I followed with Fadia and Selma to the front of the cave and took the slippery footpath down to the town. I wore thick hiking shoes, which made the grip much easier than the last time I traversed the thin path. My heart stopped every time my eyes found the darkness on either side of me, knowing that any false move could send me plummeting to my death.

Most of the lights were off in the town, but there were enough streetlights burning that I could see somebody had nailed proclamations to the side of the church, and several other buildings in town, announcing the arrival of Lord Bessinger to oversee the peaceful resolution of the cedars; of us.

"So much for the element of surprise," I said, pulling one of the posters down and crumpling it into the trash, but it was too late. There were already people huddled around the grassy knolls, fomenting and questioning what the proclamation meant.

Chapter 12

The whispers had already started by the time we reached the square. People had left their houses and were conversing on the streets, asking each other what it meant, and trying to tamp down their anxiety.

"That's them!" a young man shouted, pointing at us. "It's their fault."

An audible grumble rose from my mouth as a small group of people looked over at me.

"That makes things harder," I said, turning to Fadia. "Nur's apartment is over her bakery across the quad. Don't wait for me to get back. Take her back to the caves as fast as you can." I looked over at Selma. "You can either come with me to get Mari and my mother, or you can go with Fadia. I didn't think it would be so dangerous for you guys to come."

"I'm with you. I won't rest easy until I know that Mari is safe."

"Meanwhile, I'm sticking with the plan to get as many people on our side as possible," Leyhan said. "I'll bring them to meet at the square as soon as possible."

"Can you show Fadia the way to Nur's shop?"

"Of course."

Leyhan grabbed Fadia's hand, and they rushed across the quad as the groups of dissidents grew ever bigger. Meanwhile, I had more important things to consider, like finding my friends.

Most nights Mari slept at my mother's house. She didn't feel safe at her own home, and the memories of her past haunted her more than calmed her. I couldn't blame her. Sleeping in my old room, filled with memories of my subjugation, wasn't the most pleasant experience, but I only slept outside of my own bed for less than a week of my life, which made it easier for me. Mari had been away for over a decade. Her house didn't feel like a home when she returned to it.

I led Selma down the sinewy streets until we finally found my house. The posters hadn't been hung in my neighborhood, so the people who lived inside were blissfully unaware of what was about to descend on our sleepy little town.

I pushed open the heavy oak door to see Mari asleep on the couch in front of a dwindling fire.

"Thank the gods," I muttered, rousing Mari awake. "Time to get up. We have to go."

Mari blinked her eyes away. "Gilda?" Her head craned up to see Selma. "And Selma?"

Her face went bright red as she skittered to her feet and went to slip on the dress she had abandoned when she went to bed.

"Hi, Mari. It's great to see you," Selma said. "I wish it was under better circumstances."

"What do you mean?" Mari asked.

"Can you fill her in while I get my mother?" I asked.

Selma nodded and I dashed down the hallway, pushing open the door to my mother's room and rushing to her bed. Her room was as opulent as mine, with a big four-poster bed in the middle of it, which white linen draped down, like she was a fairy tale princess.

"Mom," I said, shaking her awake more violently than Mari because she was soundly sleeping. "Mom. Come on, get up."

"What's happ—Gilda? Oh, thank the lords you're home." She rose from her bed and hugged me. "Why are you shaking so? Did something happen?"

"*What?*" Mari shouted from the other room. "Are you kidding me?"

"You could say that, Mom," I replied. "Come on, you need to get changed. We need to go to the caves."

"What are you talking about? I'm not going to the caves, child. My old bones won't make it halfway there."

"The emperor's army is on its way here, and we need to get somewhere safe."

"The emperor's army? Why is it coming here?" She caught my eyes, and they must have told the whole story. "Oh."

"Yeah, and if we don't get you to safety, they're bound to sweep you up in this, if only to use you as a bargaining chip."

Mom nodded and scooted out of bed, dressing quickly as I watched for torches out of the front door. Finding none, I turned back to Mom as she finished tying up a bonnet.

"How do I look?"

"Not that it matters, but you look fine. Are you wearing comfortable shoes?"

She nodded. "Yes, I am."

"Good." I grabbed her hand. "Then follow me."

I brought her back to the living room, where I watched Mari and Selma embrace each other. When they heard my footsteps, they pushed away and wiped their eyes.

"Are you both ready?" I asked.

Mari nodded. "It's awful, just so awful."

"It will be okay," I said.

"What about the little ones?" Mom asked as we headed to the door. "Thorna and Bella? Who is going to them?"

"I don't think it will be a problem," I said. "They weren't supposed to be a sacrifice, so why would the army come for them?"

"They might want to bring them to another city," Mari said. "So that they can be properly sacrificed, or they might just raze the whole town. Either way, they're in danger."

"I'll handle it. What about your family?" I asked. "Do you want to warn them?"

Mari nodded. "They deserve to know."

"And what about yours, Selma?" I turned my attention to her.

"They would be on the dissidents' side I believe. Our last meeting did not end well. They can burn with the rest of the town for all I care."

I nodded. "I'm sorry to hear that. Okay, then the two of you go get Mari's family. I'm going to get Thorna and Bella. Mom, head to the caves."

"Like the dickens I am. I'm coming with you."

"It's not safe, Mom."

"That's why I'm coming. No ifs, ands, or buts about it."

I growled at her. "Fine."

Chapter 13

All the other cedars were old enough to make their own decisions without parents stepping in, but Thorna and Bella were not. Mom agreed to go find Bella while I worked on bringing Thorna and her family with me.

The lights were off when I arrived at Thorna's house. Even the embers of the fire had burned out. I banged as hard as I could on the door, attempting to rouse as many people in the house as possible. Thorna was an only child, like many cedars. The idea of losing your child didn't spring romantic ambitions in most parents.

"What?" a booming voice screamed from inside the house. A small lantern bobbed down the hallway, and when the door opened it lit a tall man with a bushy beard, wearing sleeping pajamas and a little white cap. "What do you— Gilda?"

He had every reason to be confused. It wasn't normal to storm into somebody's house in the middle of the night. "Hello, Mister Samson. I'm sorry for bothering you so late."

"Bothering is putting it lightly. You nearly gave me a heart attack. What business do you have banging on my door in the dead of night like some crazy person?"

"Again, I'm sorry, but this is urgent. I need you all to come with me to the caves where we can better protect you."

He cocked his head. "Protect us? From what?"

"Oh right. Sorry, I've done this a few times tonight already and I forget everyone's not up to speed." I told him the whole story, and when I was done, I smiled at him. "So, you see. We need you to come with us before the army gets here."

"I'm not going anywhere with you. My Thorna wasn't due to be sacrificed for another four years. She hasn't done anything wrong."

"I'm sorry." This time I was not apologetic, but indignant. "Are you saying that we did something wrong by not dying?"

"No, of course—it's Ewig who is at fault."

"For not killing us? For having an ounce of compassion?"

"That—you're twisting my words. It's late and I'm frazzled, but Thorna has done nothing wrong, and we have nothing to fear from the army."

He tried to shut the door, but I stuck my foot inside to jam it open. "Everybody in the world has something to fear from the army. Do you really think some semantic argument is going to convince them to let you go? What if they take her to another village? What if they burn her at the stake?"

"They won't do that! If they burn anyone, it will be you!"

That was it. That was the truth. I always liked Mister Samson, but now I knew the truth that he thought we should burn; that we didn't deserve to live. How could he think that, when his daughter was one of those that were supposed to burn?

"Dad?" Thorna groggily said, appearing behind her. "What are you doing?"

"Nothing, honey. Go back to bed."

"Thorna!" I shouted. "You have to come with me. The army is coming, and we need to get somewhere safe right away."

She shrugged. "Okay."

"No, dear," he said. "You aren't going anywhere with this degenerate. The last thing you need is to throw your lot in with them."

Thorna stepped forward. Something in what her father said shot through and woke her up. "My lot is already thrown in with them, or don't you remember I was supposed to burn, too?"

"Honey, I—"

"Stop it. I heard what you said. I may not have offended the emperor by refusing to die, but my lot was thrown in with them the minute I was born."

She tried to push past her father, but he threw her back onto the ground. "You will not defy me."

Thorna's face twisted with bitterness. "And what if the spots were reversed, Dad? What if I was the one that was supposed to die last year, and Gilda was the one who was next?"

"That's not what happened," Mister Samson said. "You're just a little girl. You have no idea what the world is like."

"And if you had your way, then I never would." She was crying now. "Don't you think I heard the pride in your voice when you told people I was a cedar? How do you think that made me feel, knowing my father was happy to see me die?"

"It was—"

"Horrible, Dad," she replied. "So, excuse me if I don't want to take my advice from somebody who was willing to watch me die." She stomped up to the door. "If you don't let me go, then I'll find a window, and if you lock them all, I'll cut my way through a wall with a butter knife, but I'm going."

"Let her go, Horace." The mother made an appearance. "It was our choice to let her die. We can't tell her how to live. Not now."

"Dang it, woman. Don't tell me how to raise my daughter."

"Our daughter," she replied. "And she hasn't been our daughter for 11 years. Not since we agreed to let her become a cedar. You can't claim her now, not when we already let her go."

Mister Samson dropped his shoulders, and his grip on the door. "If you step through that door, don't bother coming back."

"I won't." She grabbed her coat, and slipped on her shoes, before turning to her mother. "You can come with me."

Her mother looked at her father, then at her. "I really do love you. Be careful out there."

She bolted out the door and down the street, stifling her tears. I followed behind as the door slammed behind us. At the end of the lane, we saw Bella, crying in my mother's arms. Her parents and a little boy slightly older than Bella were trying to keep up.

"It's nice to see that at least somebody's parents care," Thorna said.

I wrapped my arms around her. "We're your family now."

She nuzzled her head into my shoulder. "You always were."

Chapter 14

Yesiburgh wasn't large, but it felt like an eternity to find our way back to the main square, darting through the streets as more and more lights turned on, and more people milled outside of their houses.

"That's them!" one hump-backed man shouted as we passed. Others barked at us too, but we didn't stop to look at them. It wasn't until we reached the square and saw a large group of people standing between us and the path up to the volcano, that I realized we were in real trouble.

"There they are!" The old woman that had accosted me in the council meeting shouted, lit by torches from the townspeople gathered around her. She turned back to her people, waving one of the posters in the air. "Do you see what I mean by them being dangerous? The emperor has sent his army to deal with us for our heathen ways!"

"Oh, thank the lords you are here." I turned to see Leyhan, who grabbed me and pulled me tight. "I'm so sorry. I thought—I really thought—"

Behind him, a small group of people, tiny enough to count on my fingers, stood. One of them was Bernice, and the red hair on three others told me it was her family.

"This is his great defense." Selma stepped through the small group toward us, with Mari wrapped around her shoulder. "Not even a tenth of their forces."

"It's not their fault," Leyhan said. "Many wanted to help but were scared off by the army."

"Can we get through the path around the mountain?"

Leyhan shook his head. "They have that blocked off, too."

"Then the only way out is through," I said. "Where are your parents?"

"They refused to see me," Mari said, sadly.

"Good riddance," Selma said with as much joy as she could squeeze out of herself.

"I agree," I said. "And what of Fadia and Nur?"

"I haven't seen them. I hope they made it back to the mountain."

"That's where we need to be, too." I stepped forward toward the square. "I'm going to talk to them."

"That's suicide."

"So is waiting for the army to find us. If I'm to die, I won't do it in silence."

I stepped forward, toward the group, as the others waited for me on the other side for a moment. Then, slowly, they stepped forward as well, until I was leading a small pond of people toward a growing ocean of them.

"If we handle them before the army gets here, then we will be heroes to them!" the old lady screamed to cheers.

"Let us through," I said, when I approached. "We mean you no harm."

"And yet, dragon meat, you bring it with every breath from your heathen mouth," the woman growled.

"We are just trying to live our lives!" Selma shouted.

"Lives ill-gotten and undeserved!" The woman stepped forward. "I always wondered why our boon was never as great as the other cities, and now we know it's because Ewig has defiled his duties by allowing you to live!"

"Technically," Mari said, "your duty is to give the great dragon lords a sacrifice. It says nothing about them eating us."

"Semantics, heathen!" the woman shouted. "Submit to our judgement and do your duty as you were born to do."

"You mean die?" I said. "You want us to die by your hand?"

"If Ewig will not do it, then we must take up arms and fulfill the will of the dragon lords."

I stomped my foot on the ground. "We will not submit to die."

"That is a shame." The crowd was quite rowdy, screaming behind her. She held up her arms and threw back her head. "We hoped you would submit to us willingly, but we will take it by force."

I balled my fists up. "You can try."

I don't know where my confidence came from. I wasn't a fighter. I wasn't a hero. I was just a scared, little girl who should have died a year ago. Maybe that was where it came from, my confidence. I should be dead already. If I died now, then what did it matter?

As the group advanced on us, a shrill voice screamed out, "STOOOOP!"

I turned to see a disheveled Sister Milka stomping across the grounds with her habit tilted to the side.

"Welcome, sister," the old woman said. "You have arrived just in time."

Sister Milka's mouth went up in a sneer. "How dare you!"

The woman was taken aback. "Excuse me, sister?"

"These are not yours to do with as you like. They are the property of the dragon lord, Ewig. We gave them to him in exchange for protection. It is not their fault they were not sacrificed. They went to their deaths with honor and grace." She stepped between us. "I know you are angry and feel betrayed. I do as well, but if you kill these women, it will do nothing but infuriate the dragon lord, and he will bring his vengeance upon us for destroying what is rightfully his."

"Let him come," somebody shouted, followed by cheers from others.

"How short sighted can you be?" Sister Milka said. "We are a peaceful town. We do not have the means for war against a dragon, let alone the emperor."

"Which is why we will burn them to avoid the emperor's retribution!" the old woman said.

"And how does the emperor feel about people taking the law into their own hands?"

The old woman's eyes went down, and the rabble calmed slightly. "Poorly."

"Exactly. He has sent in his best general to deal with this problem, and we must trust that he knows what is best. We will follow the letter of the law, as we always have, and leave our providence to the dragon lords, as it has always been."

The group grumbled, but they respected Sister Milka, at least in the matter of the cedars, and so they begrudgingly parted, and we walked through, back to the caves.

Chapter 15

The crowd grumbled and moaned as we made our way through them, but they did not attack. Sister Milka had been laid low, but she was still an authority on the dragon lords and imparted enough fear into the crowd that they kept their grubby hands off of us.

"Watch yourself," I said to my mother as I guided her past a particularly narrow passage up toward the caves above. She was not the most graceful person in the world, but she made it across with a wobbly foot.

As I let her go, I turned back to the town. The rabble still gathered at the edge, just like they did to hear Ewig's proclamation three days after their sacrifice every half decade. The whimsy was gone from their faces, the whimsy they held a year ago when I watched Ewig blow a massive fireball into the air after his statement to the crowd, and what replaced it was righteous indignation and anger.

"Fall!" the old woman shouted from the front of the group. "Do us a favor and die like you were supposed to!"

She picked up a rock and flung it through the air. It whizzed past Bella's father's face and set up a chain reaction with her followers to do the same.

"Run!" I shouted as the rocks flung through the air toward us. I pulled Leyhan behind me as we crossed the path and stumbled up the rock face toward the caves.

"They're crazy!" Leyhan shouted.

"No, they are smart to try and kill us like this," I replied. "If the mountain catches us, how can they be blamed for that?"

"They're throwing rocks at us!" he screamed, ducking from another volley. "That's not the lords' providence."

"And who's going to tell on them? Us?" I looked past the crowd to Sister Milka. She could have stopped them, said some flowery words, but she didn't. Perhaps she feared them as much as we did, or perhaps she silently prayed for our deaths as well but did not want to doom the town if they killed us.

"Stop!" Ewig's voice boomed from the top of the mountain. "Any aggression against my cedars is an aggression against me!"

Fire bellowed from his mouth across the sky, and the rocks stopped lobbing through the air. It was one thing to attack defenseless women, but quite another to anger a dragon lord who could burn down your town without breaking a sweat.

"Thank you," I said to him as I rose onto the final platform to the cave. "Is everyone okay?"

Ewig growled. "That depends on what you mean by okay."

"Gilda!" Nur's shrill voice cut through the cave and a moment later she had her arms wrapped around me. "Oh, we thought something horrible would happen to you."

"I'm so glad you are safe. Did you have any problems getting back?"

"No," Fadia said, walking up behind us. "We rushed back as quickly as we could before the group got too big. They didn't know what to do with us when we beelined past them. They seem to have coalesced once we passed. I hate that woman so much."

"She's awful," I replied. "But she's just the ringleader. They don't have to follow her."

"And without her, somebody else would step up," my mother called behind her. "Anger is always begging to be led."

We spent the next several minutes checking everything and making sure we didn't lose anyone. Except for some minor bruises from the rocks and scrapes from the climb, the group seemed to be perfectly fine, if not frazzled.

When we calmed down a moment, Renata stepped through the small corridor that led back to the dining area. "You all look a fright. Come on. I made some tea."

They looked to me for permission, and I nodded that it was okay. They began to slowly shuffle down the hallway, led by Selma and Mari, toward the dining area, as I followed behind with Ewig.

"Thank you," I said to Renata.

"Well, I don't want them here, but I'm not going to be an ungracious host either. They need to know we are not monsters."

"They are not all monsters either," I replied.

"How many came to help us?" Ewig growled as we reached his room, and he circled the fire.

I went to open my mouth, then closed it again. After a minute of thinking, I opened it more decisively. "It's not their fault. It's the posters—they are scared."

"Not many showed up then?" Renata said. "Leyhan was wrong? I'm shocked."

I nodded. "He was wrong, I'm sorry to say."

"I wish I was wrong, but I knew I wouldn't be. It's easy to give platitudes and call for equal rights for us, but it's another to put your safety on the line to fight for it."

"They don't seem to have a problem fighting against us," I said.

"That is because we threaten their truth, and their way of life. They aren't fighting against us; they are fighting for something they believe they lost."

I didn't want to believe Renata was right, but it was right there in black and white. The town let us down, and proved that no matter what they said, we would never be worth protecting. We were on our own.

Chapter 16

"I'm going back," Leyhan told me when he had finished his tea, and I was still in the middle of sipping mine. The rest of the girls, and Bella's families, were seated around the table.

"No, you're not," I replied. "I need you here."

He laughed. "That's ridiculous. You have a dragon to protect you. I need to go find more people to help us."

"You already tried it, and it didn't work. Nobody cares about us."

"That's not true." He placed his hands over mine, which were holding my tea. "You can't judge them by one harried incident."

"The old woman's people had plenty of time to foment their hatred and gather a crowd."

"Not fair," he said. "They have been gathering for weeks, waiting for a chance to act; for something to rally around. The rest of us were caught flat-footed, yes, but you can't judg—"

"YES, I CAN!" I shouted, turning all eyes to me. "Sorry, but yes I can. They chose their lot. They chose to stay on the sidelines and let us nearly be attacked."

He pulled his hands back from mine. "What about Bernice and her family? They came out for you."

"That's one family, Leyhan. Hardly says anything."

"Sure, it does. It says there is at least one family willing to fight for you. They walked out with you, ready to fight, even though they were outnumbered. Doesn't that count for anything?"

"Not enough," I replied. "And I don't want you dying for some lost cause."

He stood. "One, I'm not going to die, and two, it's not a lost cause. I'll show you."

"In just a couple of hours, the Emperor's Army is going to be in our streets," Renata said. "And then whatever embers of resolve your allies have will die."

"Excuse me if I don't believe you, Renata." He turned to the door. "But I trust in the good in people. I believe that if given the chance, they will stand for something."

"And I believe they will fall for anything," Renata said. "But I do appreciate the effort."

He ran over to me and kissed me on the cheek. "I promise I'm not going to die, and I promise that this town will prove itself to you, before the end."

I turned toward his kiss and pulled him close. "You poor, sweet boy. If you die, I'm going to kill you, understood?"

He laughed. "All the more reason to survive."

Renata rolled her eyes and growled. "If you're intent on doing this, then I suppose I should guide you down through the only path that won't lead to instant death. I set about a hundred traps to prevent the army from getting up here."

"That would be helpful." Leyhan turned to me. "I have a promise to keep, after all."

Renata led Leyhan out of the cave, and my heart broke with every step he took away from me. I didn't have much time to pine for him, though, because the moment he was out of sight, my mother touched my shoulder.

"What are we going to do now?" she asked when I turned to her. The faces of everyone in the cave screamed the same question, and I desperately wanted to have an answer for them, but I didn't.

"We're going to wait here until morning, and then, when the army comes, Ewig and I will speak to them. Depending on what they say, we'll plan from there, but please do not fear. We will protect all of you."

"And why should you get to speak to them?" Fadia asked.

"Because I am on the city council, and I speak for you in matters of the state, like this one."

My voice warbled with each word, and when I was done, I wondered what possessed me to act so confident. All eyes remained on me, and I knew it wasn't good enough, but that was all I had.

"Maybe we should all get some sleep," Mari said, standing. "We have plenty of beds upstairs..." She saw me shaking my head profusely. "Or maybe we don't."

"Come on," Fadia said. "You don't need four beds."

"Fine," Selma said. "I'll untie them, but you all owe me. We still don't have enough, though."

"What do you mean? There were like 20 last time."

"We traded some of them for essentials."

"Who would want used beds?" Mari asked.

"Some people are perverts, Mari," Selma replied, before realizing there were children present. "Sorry, but it's true."

"We still have some extra bedding, blankets and the like," Fadia said. "Nur, will you come with me to find it?"

"Of course," Nur replied, before following her up the hill.

"I think the children should sleep in the beds," Selma said, kneeling down to Bella. "You're Bella, right?"

Bella nodded. "Uh huh."

"Are you tired, sweetie?"

She yawned. "No, I'm okay."

"I have a really comfy bed up the hill. Can you take your brother and parents up to it?"

"But...I want to help."

Mari smiled. "You are helping, sweetie, by keeping your family safe, and making sure they rest."

Bella thought for a second. "Okay then."

Selma held out her hand. "Come on, I'll show you the way."

Mari and Selma fell into an easy rapport together as they took Bella's family up the hill.

"You should go, too, Mom."

"Not without you, sweetheart. I sleep when you sleep."

"That's stupid, Mom. I don't know what's going to happen, and we may have to, I don't know, walk a hundred miles, or fly on the back of a dragon."

She placed her hand on my chest. "That's why you need to rest."

I couldn't deny that the adrenaline had worn off and I was fighting my eyelids with every passing breath.

"She's right," Thorna said. "You look terrible."

"You're one to talk," I replied. "No, that's not true. You look beautiful."

Thorna's love language was insults, but I didn't have it in me to reciprocate. I was so happy to see her alive, and so heartbroken her family fed her to the wolves.

"We found three spare blankets, and a half dozen pillows," Nur said, walking back into the room with Fadia.

"I think if we clear the table, we can make a decent bed for the three of you. There are enough beds upstairs for the rest of us, except for Mari and Selma, who are going to share one."

I used to have my own bed here, but those days were gone, so I simply agreed and helped clear the table. We placed sheets on the table, and the three of us got on top of it, curling ourselves up close to each other. Before long, everyone was gone, and it was just Thorna, my mother, and I. I felt their heartbeats on either side of me, and I curled tighter into them.

"Goodnight," I said, barely able to eke out the words.

"Hey!" Renata shouted before I could drift off the sleep. "Did you know they gave away my bed?"

"Shhhh!" I replied, pulling up the blanket. "Just get in here and go to bed."

"Grrrr," Renata replied, but she didn't protest. She simply took off her shoes and curled up with us, and we drifted off to sleep, not knowing what tomorrow would bring.

Chapter 17

The next morning, I woke to the smell of bacon in the air. Renata had wrapped herself around me during the night and worked against me, trying to free herself like she hadn't been touched by another human in a long time. When I finally roused her, she spun over with a groan and I extricated myself from our cocoon, careful to avoid disturbing Thorna or my mother in the process.

"I hope you don't mind," Nur whispered as I walked gingerly to the kitchen. "It has been a while since I cooked for you girls, and I couldn't resist."

I yawned. "It's great. Smells delicious."

She sighed. "I don't know when I'm going to get another chance to eat a home-cooked meal." She pointed to the tunnel that led to the smokehouse. "Fadia has been packing up all our excess meat and gathering everything we can carry."

I nodded. "That's for the best, I think. What about the gems?"

The volcano was filled with precious gems embedded on every wall. Since the area wasn't settled until Ewig tamed the volcano, nobody knew about it until he had already taken residence, and he hoarded his wealth...well, like a dragon.

"Mari and Selma are going to mine as much as they can, and we'll show the others how to do so as well."

"Do you really think we'll have to leave?" I asked.

She shrugged. "I have no idea, but I want to be prepared for anything. Better to have it and not need it than the opposite."

"And Ewig is okay with you destroying his cavern by stripping its gems?"

"What he doesn't know won't hurt him." She slid a boiling pot of tea toward me and a cup. "I think you like dandelion tea, if I remember."

"I do," I said. "It reminds me of my youth."

She laughed loud enough to echo through the cave, and then caught herself. "Sorry, but you are still just a child."

"If that's true, this is a lot to put on a child."

She nodded. "You're right. You shouldn't have to be the conduit between our two worlds, but then, none of us should have been sacrificed in the first place."

"We all have our curses to bear."

I poured the tea and took a deep sip. As the tea coated my throat, I thought back to the years when I didn't know better and couldn't comprehend that one day I would be devoured by the dragon lord, Ewig. He was such an imposing figure in my life. I thought him boundlessly powerful, but last night, he looked as scared as the rest of us. I did not want to meet the monsters who could scare a dragon lord, but that was exactly what I would do today.

"Maybe Renata should be the one to meet with Lord Bessinger," I said as I took another sip of tea.

"Are you kidding? She's as likely to jab him through the throat as he is to do the same to her, and then where would we be?

"No, your instinct was right. It needs to be you. You are on the town council, and you speak for us, professionally, with them. If they will listen to anyone, it's you."

"Bacon!" Bella yelled as she ran into the cave. She ran over to the cooking table and hopped onto my lap as Nur slid a plate over to her. "This is for everyone, so go easy, and it's very hot, so be careful."

She either didn't hear her, or heard her and didn't care, because she grabbed a big piece and ripped a piece off with a big smile. She had barely bit down on it when she let out a howl. "Ow, it's hot!"

"I told you." Nur held out her hand. "Spit."

Bella spit the piece out and placed the bacon on the table. She was not good with impulse control, and every second she had to wait to watch it cool was agony. After a few seconds, it had cooled enough that she could pop it back into her mouth.

With Bella's entrance, the entire cave started to come back alive. My mother roused, followed by Thorna, and finally Renata. By the time they gathered around the table, Mari and Selma had made their way down to the cave with Fadia, with Bella's family pulling up the rear.

It was a strange feeling, being around them all, and feeling safe and warm in their company, while still being petrified of what was to come at the same time. We should have gotten together like this more often, when the world wasn't baring its teeth at us. I never brought Thorna or Bella up to the encampment, not because I feared anything, but because I didn't think about it.

I wasn't hungry, but I swallowed down two pieces of bacon and a bowl of oatmeal before I took my tea and climbed the stairs toward Ewig's keep.

"Hey," Renata said. "Don't do anything I would."

"I don't intend on it. If everyone leaves this meeting with their heads, I will consider it a win."

"Low bar, but an accurate one, unfortunately," Renata said. "Don't die."

"Seconded!" Thorna shouted.

"Here here!" the group chanted.

"Is that really possible? For you to die?" my mother asked, running up to me. "Is it really that dangerous?"

"I don't think so," I said. "After all, I have a dragon, remember?"

My mother grabbed me tight. "You're right. Just stay behind him, alright?"

"I'll do what I can."

I humored her long hug before finally breaking free and heading across the rope bridge. When I entered Ewig's room, he was not there, and his fire had died out. I found him at the edge of the cave, looking out onto the horizon.

"Have you been here all night?"

"No, just the last hour or so," he said.

The horizon was filled with gleaming metal and red cloth, filling in the break in the canopy several miles away. "I can see why."

"Quite," he replied. "They're here."

I knew it was coming, but I still couldn't believe it, even after seeing it with my own eyes.

Chapter 18

The soldiers arrived at the edge of town by mid-morning, waving the emperor's red and yellow colors proudly on either side of their party as they marched. We couldn't make out what they were doing, but by the time they reached the center of town, a crowd had gathered, both in the town and behind us, with all the residents of the cave, new and old, peering over us.

"What do you think they are doing?" Thorna asked, using my shoulders to press herself up to get better leverage.

A small cadre of townspeople walked to the center of the square and met with the army officers.

"I don't know. I'm not a diplomat."

Ewig growled. "They are presenting themselves to the town elders, in this case the city council. I would bet right around now they are learning you are not only a cedar, but a deserter to your post."

"Fabulous. Just what I need; another reason for them to cut off my head."

Eventually, the tête-à-tête finished at the center of town. The groups disbanded to their opposite sides of the quad, except for one soldier, who made their way through the crowd, toward us.

At the edge of the path, the soldier took off their helmet to reveal long, blonde hair. They placed their helmet on the edge of town, as well as their sword, presenting it first into the air before resting it on the ground.

"They are showing us they are unarmed." Ewig turned back to the others. "You should go somewhere safe."

The group of cedars and their families marched through the cave and back to the dining area, except for me, who stayed by Ewig's side as he stood up straight to welcome his uninvited guest.

"Do your best not to speak," he growled at me.

"It's going to be hard, since they are here to decide my fate."

"No, this isn't about you."

"I find that hard to believe."

He sighed. "This is about me defying my family. You have done nothing wrong, and I will make that abundantly clear."

I had to admit, that was a bit of a relief. I thought for sure I would be bound and shackled for simply existing. Not that Ewig being in trouble was a pleasant thought, but it was a right bit better than being in trouble myself and fearing death.

The closer the soldier got, the more I noticed her soft face, and bright blue eyes which seemed larger than possible, given the size of her face.

When she finally pulled herself up to our level and stood in front of us, there was no laboring on her breath. She simply shook off her hair and then stood crisply at attention.

"Dragon lord Ewig, my apologies for my appearance This is not the easiest path to traverse."

Ewig growled. "There are many things you should apologize for, but your appearance is not one of them."

"And where do these apologies begin?"

"First among them, where is Lord Bessinger, and why has he not come to greet me personally?"

"You are right." She bowed. "My apologies, Your Majesty. He is eager to speak with you but climbing such a height is unbecoming of one of his stature. He is an old man, you see, and would prefer to see you in the town square, where both your safety is assured."

"Safety!" I scoffed. "I nearly died in that crowd last night."

Ewig's tail tapped me on the back, and I remembered that I wasn't supposed to speak, so I swallowed my tongue.

She cocked her head. "That is most unfortunate, but I promise none would do you harm, especially with a dragon on your side."

"What is your name?" Ewig asked.

"Of course. How rude of me. They call me Dame Farcile. I am a general in the Emperor's army."

"You look quite young to be a general," Ewig said, with as much condescension as I ever heard from him.

"In fairness, great dragon, all humans look young to you, I am sure."

"True, but you are young even for your kind."

She smiled. "I have brought the crown many great victories in my few years. I assure you, I earned my post."

"I do not deny it. I am simply stating a fact. It was not meant as a slight."

"And I didn't take it as such."

Ewig's mouth crested into a light smile, revealing rows of sharp, white teeth. "Can we please agree not to lie to each other? It will make this go much smoother, and it is only in honesty that we can build truth."

She cleared her through. "Quite. You are right, I was insulted by it. I'm sorry. I have had to defend my age for a long time against many, friend and foe alike."

"And are we friend or foe?"

"I certainly hope friend, Your Grace."

"I hope so too," Ewig said. "Now, you can go back to your commander and tell him that, while I appreciate his invitation, I would prefer he come to me."

She cleared her throat. "Oh my, this is awkward. First, I would like you to know that I hold you in the highest reward, lord Ewig, but I must inform you that this was not a request, though I have couched it as such."

Flames puffed from his nostrils. "Are you demanding I lower myself to the requests of humans?"

"No, sir," Dame Farcile said. "I would never presume as such."

"Then on whose authority do you act if not the emperor's?" I asked. "Because unless I have been misinformed, he is still a human."

"I'm afraid our authority comes from a higher power."

"And who is more powerful than the emperor?" I asked.

"Ramidion," Ewig growled. "That is who summons me, is it not?"

Dame Farcile nodded. "That is correct. We are under direct authority of the dragon lord, Ramidion, and Lord Bessinger speaks for her in all matters. His words are her words and denying him is denying her."

Ewig's eyes narrowed. "Leave now, before I lose my temper, and tell your Lord I will see him presently."

Chapter 19

There was a tense stand-off between Dame Farcile and Ewig, one which I thought would surely end with her charred corpse tumbling down the mountain, but after some tense seconds, the General simply nodded and spun on her heels, before making her way down the mountain. I didn't say anything until she was safely back in town.

"You can't be serious about going down to the town that was ready to kill me a few hours ago."

"I am," he replied. "And you are staying here."

I laughed, not because his words were particularly funny, but out of nervousness. "There is no way I'm letting you go into that hornet's nest alone."

"My job is to protect you, all of you."

"And you can't do that if you're dead."

Now it was his turn to laugh. "Please, there is nothing alive that can kill me, save for the talons of my brothers and sisters. I can assure you, Ramidion would never part with one of them, lest she make herself vulnerable to attack as well. I'll be fine."

"And when was the last time you left this cave? There could have been something new they've found since the last time you visited the outside world. You have no idea—"

"And you have no idea what my sister is capable of."

"Yes, I do. I've read about her in books. She started the war on the gods and won our freedom."

Ewig blew smoke out of his nose. "That is certainly what she wants you to believe, but the truth is more complicated than that."

"Then what is the truth?"

He turned away from me. "She did start a war on the gods, but not for some noble goal of winning freedom, for herself or others. She wanted power and wasn't happy being the second most formidable being on the planet. So, she decided to remedy that fact."

"I don't bel—"

He spoke over me. "I was there, Gilda, when she devised her plan, and set out to convince the humans to join with her. She knew the gods drew power from humanity, and that many were left behind by their predilections. She played on that feeling to turn the powerful to her side, promising them wealth and freedom in exchange for their help bringing down the gods. Without humanity's worship to give them power, the gods lost their power, which Ramidion and her allies used to drive them from Earth."

"And in doing so, supplant their power with hers."

"Now you begin to understand." Ewig nodded. "She is smarter than us all, and shrewd. I hoped she would turn her eyes away when she found out the truth. I thought we were remote, and obscure. News of my misdeeds wouldn't matter here, but I was wrong. She considers any deviation from her will as a slight against her power that must be squashed with extreme prejudice."

"Which is why she is using the might of her army."

"Yes. She must show everyone what happens when you disrespect her." He turned back to me. "I don't know what she will do to me, and I don't know what will happen without my protection, but if the worst happens, do what you can to survive. Take as many gems as you can carry. I have kept some of the best treasures hidden under the fire I have burned for so many years. They should fetch you a good price on the market. Don't hesitate. Without me, I don't know what they will do."

I stepped toward him, placing my hand on his leathery wing. "I can't let you go down there alone. I won't. I was chosen to speak for the cedars, and I will not allow you to be taken without a fight."

"A fight is exactly what they want, Gilda. Haven't you been listening? They are at their most powerful in a fight. Might makes right with my sister, and the emperor, and they are mighty."

"She's right," Renata said, coming out from the darkness.

"Don't you come into this, too," Ewig growled. "Don't you understand what—"

"Just listen, you big lug," Renata said. "We need time to get away. We aren't done packing yet. The longer you can keep them distracted, the more time we have to flee this place."

"You can't be serious about leaving," I said.

"I hope it doesn't come to that, but there's got to be a town across the lake that will give us clemency. Somewhere the dragon lords can't touch."

"They don't touch the outskirts because there is nothing there that interests them, but they are very interested in you," I said. "You will be on the run for the rest of your lives if you leave this place."

"And if we stay, then we will be forced to succumb to the emperor's law which says we are destined to die."

"Then you must leave," Ewig said. "The gems will be currency anywhere you go, but be careful because they will track you everywhere, and use them as a trail to lead them to you if you let them."

Ewig's keep was at the edge of the world, but there were places past it, across the lake from his forbidden forest, which were untouched by the dragon lords; small pockets of freedom that did not fall under Ramidion's rule.

"Then at the very least," I said, "let me negotiate for them. Even if there is nothing I can do for you, let me do it for them. Maybe I can earn their freedom."

Ewig growled for a long moment. "Fine, you can come. You are a pain, did you know that?"

I turned to Renata. "We'll hold them off as long as possible. Give you time to evacuate. If I don't come back by the time you are ready, go."

Renata grabbed my hands. "Do you remember where I taught you how to fish?"

"You mean where you almost killed Leyhan?"

"That too." She dropped her eyes. "We'll wait for you there as long as we can, but if we see soldiers coming over the ridge, we will have to leave."

"Set as many traps along the way as you can," Ewig said. "Trip them up. They are powerful but lumbering. You have the advantage in the trees, as long as you don't stop."

Renata squeezed my hands. "Don't die."

"I'll do my best," I replied, pulling my hands away.

"Come on," Ewig said, lowering his wings. "Hop on. We have to go. If they demand I engage with them on their terms, then I intend to make a show of my power before I kowtow to them."

Chapter 20

Ewig's wings were hard and leathery, with thick bones wrapped tightly under them, which gave me a foothold to climb onto his back. His back looked smooth from a distance, but up close I felt every scale as I rubbed my hand across them.

"We don't have all day," he said.

"Right," I replied, wrapping my hand against the hard, black bone that made up the jagged protrusions down his spine. Those I always thought would be sharp, but they were smooth, like teeth, and when I wrapped my legs around them, the scales held me tightly, preventing me from sliding off either side.

"I haven't had a rider on my back since the war," Ewig grumbled. "And even then, he had a harness."

"Do I need a harness?" I asked in a panic, my heart pounding in my ears.

"Whether you do or not, we don't have time to find one, and even if we did, I vowed to never be saddled again." He kicked off the ground and my stomach dropped to my pelvis as with one flap of his wings we shot into the air. It only took a few seconds before we were above the volcano, and I could look down directly into the caldera.

"Man was not meant to soar this high," I said, wrapping my arms even tighter around the dragon's spine spikes.

"You worry too much, pet," Ewig replied, his words lighter than I ever heard them before. "This is true freedom."

He twisted himself in a circle. I felt myself rise from the seat on the dragon lord's back for a moment, before an invisible hand pushed me back into my seat as he righted himself.

"How did you like that?"

It was hard to explain, because while there was great fear in his acrobatics, there was an amazing thrill in it as well. It was at the same time terrifying and exhilarating in a way I had never felt before.

"I think I liked it," I replied, surprised at the smile that crept across my face.

"If you liked that, wait until you see this!"

I belted myself down until my whole body gripped the scales of his back, and he rose high into the air, making a long backward loop with his body that carried us into another complete circle, all without him twisting his body at all.

I screamed as the invisible hand of the universe pushed me from Ewig's back, and then, an instant later, snapped me back when we leveled off again.

"How was that one?" Ewig said. "Nadar always liked that one best."

"Was that your rider?" I asked.

"They were," he replied. "Until Eirsoffa blew them off my mount in a particularly bloody battle. I never chose another for the rest of the war."

We had read stories about how Emperor Paraphal I was once Ramidion's rider, and as a reward for his service, she installed him as emperor after the war.

The dragon riders were the greatest champions among the humans, and their bond with the dragons exemplified the bond between the dragon race and humanity. When they bled, we bled, and together, we banished the gods.

Sister Milka believed it was mostly a ceremonial position to keep the humans fighting, and that they were a mostly unnecessary part of the war. After gripping tight to Ewig's back for the past several minutes, I had to agree with her. It would be impossible to be an effective fighter when the wind whipped at you so for daring to stand against it.

"I can see why one would need a saddle to sit upon you in battle."

"Nadar was an expert with a bow," Ewig said. "He found ways to use the wind to his advantage by firing backwards and using our momentum to fire his weapon at incredible speed."

I turned my head slightly, and felt the wind whip past me, blowing incredibly fast as we cut through the air. Yes, I saw how that could be beneficial.

"When are we going to land?"

"Are you so sick of the air now?"

I shook my head. "No, it's not that." But it was. My stomach rose and fell with every small correction in the dragon's flight, and I felt as though I would lose my breakfast if I stayed airborne much longer. "I just think we don't want to make Lord Bessinger any angrier."

"That is where you are wrong," Ewig said. "We must make a show of it, lest he think we will kowtow to his every order. Powerful beings work on their own schedule." He looked down. "However, I suppose it is time to show my force, and make my presence known."

He tilted himself down, and we dove down to the town below. My stomach flipped and turned as my head grew lighter and the whole of the ground began to spin under me.

We ducked under the clouds, toward the square under us. A congregation of fifty soldiers stood at attention at one end near the school, while citizens lined either side of it. As we neared the ground, the villagers screamed out, pointing to us as if we were about to attack. They took cover wherever they could, while the soldiers stood firmly, unmoving and unflinching.

At the last moment, Ewig extended his wings and pulled up, leveling off above the square and swooping up into the air. As he did, he opened his mouth and fire poured out of it, covering the air with a thick cloud of flames and smoke.

His momentum carried him higher, and when he peaked, he used his wings to float down to the square, in front of the church, as people vacated to make room for him.

When he was on the ground, he stomped his feet and once again sprayed a heavy layer of fire into the air, and it rained down onto the square. The villagers worked to stomp out the embers, while the military again stayed still, focused, and determined.

As the fire rained down, Ewig stepped forward. "You wanted to see me, General? Well, here I am."

Chapter 21

Lord Bessinger was a massive mountain of a man who towered over the others behind him, made even more stark by the solid gold plate mail armor he wore, etched with the symbol of the emperor in red on his chest and shoulder pauldrons.

"It's good to finally meet you, Lord Ewig." His voice was raspy, like he ate glass that cut up his throat. "It has been a long time since the Gilded Army had the pleasure of an audience with you."

"Since your grandfather became my sister's lapdog," he replied. "I see you have joined a long line of sycophants."

When he stepped forward, Dame Farcile took a step as well, but he stayed her from joining him with a firm hand and continued on by himself. "I don't work for your sister. I am loyal to the crown, and Emperor Paraphal."

"Is that why you invoked my sister's name, and not her pet?" Ewig scoffed. "You can stop hiding behind your emperor. I know who you truly speak for."

"I see my general loosened her tongue."

"Don't look badly on her," Ewig said. "I am a shrewd negotiator."

"Yes, I have been told as much, though your sister used the word stubborn instead." Lord

Bessinger took another step forward. "We thought it the only way to make you see how serious we were. We know how you feel about humanity." His eyes tracked to me from under his helmet. "Or, we thought we did."

"Just because I do not want to kill the humans who are sacrificed in my name, does not mean that I like them any more than I once did."

"Is that so? Because I heard you let them live with you, in your keep, which seems to betray your feelings."

"Do you keep servants, Lord Bessinger, in your many castles?"

He nodded. "Of course I do. We would not get by without them."

"The same is true for me. I chose this place, far from the bustle of the capitol, to live in solitude. However, what I did not realize was that, in order to take care of my basic needs, creature comforts if you will, I needed humans who could tend farms, hunt, and keep my cave in the way I had become accustomed."

What was he saying? That we were nothing but servants to him? But I knew that wasn't true. He cared for me, for us. I knew he did. Why would he treat us with such kindness if he didn't care at all? Despite asking for his meals, he never bothered us with any other requests.

He took another step forward. "Had you come to the crown, we would have arranged that for you."

"You must know of the bad blood between my sister and me. There was no way I would ask her for a favor." He looked around, growling. "I had become accustomed to living on my own, in the heat of the volcano, when this town, Yesiburgh, sprung up around me, worshipped me, and as such, continued the tradition that my sisters and brothers forced upon humanity. Suddenly, I was awash with servants, every five years like clockwork, and I decided to do what I will with them."

"That is not in the spirit of the law."

"I disagree." He cleared his throat. "They have sacrificed their lives to me and live at my beck and call. At any time, I can call on my life debt, and take their souls, but I have seen no need to do so as of yet."

Lord Bessinger growled. "That is not how the Black Charter is worded."

"I know the words as much as you," Ewig said. "It's actually not spoken about what I am to do with them. My sister should have made it clearer if she wanted to force their murder. I would very much prefer lapdogs for decades than a single, stringy snack that would barely satiate me a week."

"The implication of the Black Charter is—"

"Is nothing!" Ewig's voice boomed across the square, sending shivers down my spine. In the silence that followed, I tracked my eyes across the crowd, looking for Leyhan in the familiar faces around me. He should have been out, front and center, but instead, he was nowhere to be found, even buried deep behind the others. "It is not explicitly stated what needed to be done with the villagers who were sacrificed to me. If my sister demanded that I eat them, then she should have placed that in her original edicts. As they are written now, these girls are mine to do as I so choose, and as such I have put them to work, tending my keep."

Lord Bessinger thought for a long moment, and removed the gilded helmet from his head, storing it in the crook of his arm. Again, his eyes found me. "Is that why you allowed this one to ride on your back?"

"Gilda," I said. "My name is Gilda."

"Your name is inconsequential. Dead girls don't have names, and by the laws of the land, you should no longer draw breath, and so, to me, you do not exist."

"Do not insult me," I replied, stepping forward. "I am on the city council and speak for Ewig in matters related to the town. That is how I serve my master, and I will not have you speak ill of him."

"I do not speak ill of him, but of you."

"And as his property, that is the same thing," Ewig said. "If you speak ill of her, you speak ill of me, and you know how much we dragons value our honor."

"Is that a threat?" Lord Bessinger growled.

"Not a threat. Just a statement. I will not insult my sister's property, and her property can do me the same courtesy."

"I am NOT her property," Lord Bessinger growled.

"You wear her sigil," Ewig said. "You speak her words. It is the same thing."

He lowered his eyes. "I have not come here to fight, but to resolve this without bloodshed."

"Yet, you bring an army with you."

"Not an army, a small battalion of peacekeepers."

"Your elite force, by the looks of it," Ewig growled. "It has been a long time, but I recognize the armor of my sister's best troops." He stopped for a moment. "But if you truly come in peace, then I will welcome you with friendship. I invite you and your general to dinner at my keep tonight. We will break bread, and you will tell me your terms of friendship."

He shook his head. "I won't be doing that."

Ewig's lip twitched. "That wasn't a request. The only other option is that I burn you alive right here, and your men along with you, for having the audacity to command me."

"And you would cause a war, the eleven other houses against yourself."

"It has been a long time, but you must have heard how spiteful I can be." Ewig took a step forward and the earth shook under him. "Do you truly think I would not welcome a fight to smite my enemies?"

For the first time, I saw a flicker of fear in Lord Bessinger's eyes. It only lasted a fleeting second, but it was as clear as the nose on his face. After a moment, he recovered, and stood straight up.

"Very well," he said. "We shall arrive promptly at nightfall."

"Excellent. I am so glad you are not so scared of me that you refuse my hospitality." Ewig tipped his wing down. "Come, Gilda. We must prepare."

"Oh," Lord Bessinger said. "And before you think about misbehaving tonight..." He snapped his fingers and the squad parted. From it two soldiers brought forward a beaten and bruised man. When his eyes connected with mine, I saw my beautiful Leyhan. "Know that this town will suffer greatly if you do, starting with this boy."

Chapter 22

"NO!" I shouted. "What have you done to him?"

"Me?" Lord Bessinger said. "Nothing. Some concerned citizens saw that he was trying to raise a militia against the emperor's army, and brought him before me, like this. Why? Do you know him?"

I sneered. "You know I do."

"I have heard he is your beloved." He furrowed his brow. "I am sorry for using such a dirty, low tactic, but I need you both to know that we have eyes everywhere, and know everything, and if every person you are hiding in that cave is not present at our little meeting tonight, I will make life very uncomfortable for this town, starting with your precious lover."

I rushed forward, ready to fight, but Ewig's wing lifted into the air to hold me back. "Wait, Gilda. If you strike him, there is nothing I can do to protect you, or Leyhan."

Lord Bessinger smiled. "Listen to your precious dragon lord and let the adults handle this."

I tried to fight against Ewig's leathery wings, but it was useless. When I wouldn't get onto his back willingly, he grabbed me effortlessly with his talons and swooped into the air. Without the theatrics, it wasn't five minutes back to the cave, and when he landed, he tossed me onto the ground.

"You should have let me hit him," I growled as I stood.

"Then you would endanger yourself, and everyone that we strive to protect."

"I know," I said, my heart rate slowing. "I know, but it would have felt really good."

"For a moment, and then you would have a lifetime of regret. Trust me, you do not want Ramidion as your enemy. You barely want her as your friend, and even then, you need to watch your back for arrows and daggers at every turn."

"Is she really that ruthless?" I asked.

"Moreso. She was ruthless a hundred years ago. Now, she is something else entirely. She believes everyone, especially her family, are after the power she clings to, and is looking for any reason to snuff us out."

"Then what do we do?" I asked as I walked back with him toward his keep.

"Entertain him with a splendid dinner, just like the old days." He thought for a second. "Do you think the dining area is big enough for a full-grown dragon?"

I nodded. "I think we can make room."

"Good," he said, curling up. "Then I will leave you to it. The day is already upon us, so I suggest you get going."

"I will." I started toward the cave tunnel, but before I disappeared into it, I turned back to him. "All that stuff you said, about us being your servants. That was all an act, right?"

He chortled to himself. "You would be the worst servants of all time. I don't think you have ever listened to a thing I said, and the others are even worse. An untrained fox would be more helpful."

"I love you, too, Ewig."

"And wear something nice for dinner, not those rags."

"These are nice..." I started, but even I couldn't defend them. I had been wearing the same plain red dress for a week and it started to show its wear.

He growled in response as I continued through the cave into the dining area. Everyone was bustling around, preparing food, and mining for as many precious gems as they could pull from the walls of the cave.

"She's back!" Thorna shouted as I hopped down the stairs. "I knew she wouldn't die."

Nur smiled at me. "I guess I owe you a gold coin, then."

I hugged Thorna and then Nur in turn, before turning to Renata. "We need to prepare for a feast."

"That's stupid. Why would we do that?"

"Because Ewig invited Lord Bessinger and his general here for a meal, and we need to make it a meal fit for a king."

"That's insane," Fadia said. "I don't have that kind of supply, and even if I did, we need it for travel."

"We can't travel," I said.

"Why?" Renata said. "That was the whole plan."

"Because Lord Bessinger told us he had soldiers watching our every move, and if we move, he's going to destroy the town."

"So?" Thorna said. "Screw them."

I turned back to her. "I'm not going to kill a bunch of innocent people so we can escape. I can't have that on my conscience."

"Innocent?" Mari said. "They tried to kill you literally last night."

"A small group, but not all of them. Besides...they have Leyhan."

"Oh no," Selma said. "I'm sorry, Gilda. I know how much he means to you."

"To all of us. Even if there's not one other decent person in that town, Leyhan has always tried to protect us, to help us, even after you all tried to kill him."

"I'm not denying that," Renata said. "But it's one life against all of ours, and let's be honest here, there's a pretty good chance he's as good as dead."

"Be that as it may," I replied, "I'm not leaving until he's safe."

"That's your choice," Selma said.

"It's mine too," Mari said.

"I will stay with my fellow baker," Nur said.

"You are the worst," Fadia said.

"Even if we do leave," my mother said, "what's to stop them from following us and slitting our throats when we're far enough from Ewig's protection? Here we may be trapped, but at least we're safe."

"We don't even know what Lord Bessinger is going to say, anyway. He might just want Ewig."

"And what?" Renata said. "We just give him to the army?"

"Of course not," I replied. "But we need to hear what he has to say."

"The longer we stay here," Renata said, "the more likely they are to be able to trap us. I don't know what Lord Bessinger's plan is, but he didn't get to lead the army without being a good tactician. If we're going to stay, we need a plan as good as his."

"I'm working on it," I replied. "Everyone think on it, but until we have one, we need to act like everything is fine, which means, Nur, start cooking."

"Just like old times." Nur smiled.

"Maybe we can poison his food," Bella said.

"That's a horrible thing to say," Renata replied with a smile. "It's not a bad plan, though."

"I'll take it under advisement, but he's just the tip of the spear, remember? The last thing we need is to kill the general and become public enemy #1."

"Plan B, then?" Selma asked.

"How about Plan J?" I replied.

"As long as it's on the docket," Selma replied with a smile, walking over to help Nur with the food.

Chapter 23

When did I become the leader of these people? Did it happen a little bit at a time, or all at once? I agreed to a seat on the council to speak for them, but that felt more like being beholden to them, not above them, and yet now I was flying off into a meeting with Ewig and telling them what to do to prepare for negotiation. I was arguing against them fleeing and telling them to trust me with their lives.

What if I was unworthy of that trust? What if I was wrong, and they got slaughtered for believing in me? What if they were dragged in front of the great dragon Ramidion, and burned for the crime of existing? I couldn't help but notice my moral compass spun wildly in my stomach, making me nauseous.

The thought of all of it crashed upon me at once, and I rushed out of the dining area as the others rushed around, preparing for the feast. They pulled jerky from their stores, and Renata took Fadia down to the garden to pick as many fresh fruits and vegetables as they could carry. Bella's parents joined them to give extra hands, while Bella worked with Thorna to gussy up the room and make it seem fitting for a feast.

But I couldn't help. My chest was heavy, and my breath labored as I struggled my way up into the bedroom and collapsed on the floor. I didn't expect the tears to come, nor that when they came, they would fall so thick and heavy from my face as I rested my face on the dirt ground.

"Are you oka—" My mother entered the door, grasping the edge of the cave. When she saw me, her face sank and she knelt in the dirt with me, rubbing my back. "My poor baby. What's wrong?"

"I can't, ma—" I huffed in air to get the strength to speak. "I ca—it's too much."

She grabbed me and pulled me into her bosom, where I sobbed and sobbed until her shirt was soaked with my tears.

"I know. It's too much. It's all too much. It's not fair."

I took a deep breath. "Nothing in my life has been fair, from the moment I came out of the womb." I tilted my head toward hers, and my red eyes found her face. "I shouldn't even be alive right now."

"No," she replied. "But I'm so glad you are, and I think that might be the first fair thing that has happened for us in a long time."

My head tilted down again. "Lot of good it did. Look at us. Trapped in a cave while the army closed in around us. A town that reviles us, and these people count on me, and I feel like I'm letting them down."

"Oh, sweetheart." She rubbed my head. "I'm sure you are, in some ways."

"Thanks, Mom."

"That came out wrong. What I meant was that we all fail the ones we love every now and then. Often in irreparable ways. Look at me. I could have left you with your father, and you would be free of this right now, or maybe you would be dead."

"I—again, not helpful."

"I just mean all we can do is what we think is best. I believed that by not taking you away to live in the woods, you would have a better life, even if it was shorter, than I did when I was your age. Was I right? No, but I only realized that too late. It came from a place of love, and that's all we can do."

"You were so wrong," I said.

"I know, but I wasn't much older than you when I had you, and your father wasn't either. Do you think you are equipped to handle something huge like that right now?"

"Lord, that is depressing," I said. "I don't think I'm equipped to tie my own shoes most days."

"Exactly, and yet we were expected to raise a child, a child that everybody in the whole town, in the whole world, expected to die for the good of the world." She swallowed. "But this isn't about me. It's about you."

"Well, in fairness, that was pretty much about me. I was the one that was supposed to die, after all."

"True," she said, before stopping for a moment. "What we expect of the young isn't fair.

It's not fair at all, and it's especially unfair to you."

When I looked up, I saw the tears welling in her eyes. "I'm just saying that we can't know if the decisions we made are good or bad in the moment, maybe not even years later. I let you go to your death, hoping for the best, and you came back to me, like my little miracle. All we can do is what we think is right, and hope for the best. If you are coming from a place of love, then that's all you can do."

"I think I am," I said. "I just don't want to fail them, like so many people failed me."

"You won't fail them," she said. "I won't let you."

"That's comforting," I said with a smile. "Weren't you just telling me how badly you failed me?"

She chuckled, but with a sad moan after it. "And yet, here you are, laying in my arms, trusting me to care for you still."

"Ah," I said, finally realizing what she was trying to tell me. "Thank you, Mom. That was really helpful for a big failure."

"Well, I have a lot of experience with the subject." She kissed my forehead. "I am glad it resonated."

Chapter 24

I felt much better after taking some time to have a mental breakdown.

"Are you sure you're okay?" my mother asked as she wiped the last of the tears from my eyes.

I nodded. "I think so."

"Good." She slid aside to reveal Mari standing behind her at the entrance to the cave. "Because we have a lot of work to do."

"What's that supposed to mean?"

"We're having guests, and that means you can't look like a homeless beggar," Selma said.

I looked down at my red dress. "I think I look nice."

"Oh honey," my mother said. "I love you, but you look a fright, and look at your hair."

"Come with us," Mari said. "We need to fix this quickly if you want Lord Bessinger to take you seriously."

"I already negotiated with him in this," I said in a huff. "It's fine."

"Yes, exactly," Mari said. "It's fine, and that's not good enough."

I didn't have it in me to fight any more, so I allowed Mari and Selma to lead me up to the baths above the bedroom. Mari left me to soak in one of the hot springs as Selma went about trimming my hair and removing the flyaways so that I looked less like a scared child and more like an esteemed city councilor.

"I can't believe we let you represent us looking like this," Selma said, shaking her head.

"I am a human, you know, and I can hear you. You could stand to be a little nicer."

"And you could stand to be a little meaner. Do you even know anything about Lord Bessinger?"

"Well, no. But I know about the army."

"He's not just the leader of the army," Selma said. "He's their most brutal general. He's absolutely ruthless. He would rather raze a city to the ground than allow them to surrender. He thinks the only way to control people is through fear, and that is his game: control. He looks for any weakness in his opponents, and then exploits them."

"That sounds like a brutal person I have no interest in being around."

"And you shouldn't. Still, Ewig and he have something in common, being as they were both forged in war."

"Was Ewig really as bloodthirsty as Lord Bessinger?"

"Once, long ago, yes. He was every bit the monster Lord Bessinger is, or worse."

"I couldn't imagine Ewig being like that."

"A year ago, you thought he was going to eat you alive."

"Yeah, but I've known him for a year now, and I can't imagine him being a psychotic killer."

"He was once a dog of the military, like Lord Bessinger, and you don't kill as many people as Ewig did without being a bit psychotic. You don't fight the gods if you don't have a complex."

"I guess."

"Are you still working?" Mari re-entered the room as Selma sheared my hair on the right side. "Or are you just gabbing now?"

"A little of both." Selma tapped my shoulders. "Turn around."

I did as she said, and when I spun to her, she stared at me for a long moment. "Looks just about perfect. Some of my best work."

"Good," Mari said. "Because I finished the alterations."

She held up a deep blue dress with gold stitches embroidered into the breast, weaving through the seams like vines on a trellis.

"It's beautiful," I said, standing from the spring and drying myself off. Wiping off the gross from the last few days made me feel like a new woman. "Did you just sew this?"

She laughed. "Are you sure you're Odine's daughter? It would take weeks to stitch something this complicated. I made it while I lived here, but I'm a little bit bigger than you, so I had to take it in."

When I was done toweling myself off, Selma and Mari helped me into the dress. First the undergarments, then the corset, until finally the dress slid over my shoulders. Selma finished my hair with a golden headband, and a glass rose that she placed behind my ear.

When I finally glanced at myself in the mirror, I looked like a noblewoman, something I hadn't been able to pull off since I was—well, ever. Even after coming home, I didn't feel comfortable in the dresses my mother made, and so I stayed mostly in flowing gowns that let me move.

"Thank you," I said, nearly breathless, from both the sight of myself and the tightness of my corset.

"Don't eat too much," Selma said. "Otherwise, you'll hurt yourself."

"And sit up straight," Mari said. "Not that you have much choice. If you slouch, you'll hurt yourself."

"I get it. I'm probably going to hurt myself," I said. "Do you think I'm ready?"

"Absolutely not," Selma said. "But you have no other choice."

"Thanks for the vote of confidence," I replied.

"Weren't you just broken down on the floor of this room a couple hours ago, convinced you were going to get us all killed?"

"Yes, but that was me saying it, not somebody else."

Selma placed her hands on my shoulders. "Whatever you do, don't get us killed. Please."

Chapter 25

I didn't have a plan.

I told them I would formulate a plan, but I still couldn't think straight. All I could do was go through the motions as Selma cut my hair and Mari dressed me. I told them to stay in the caves and that I would protect them. Now, in the moment of truth, I didn't have anything except to put one foot in front of the other and hope for the best.

My only saving grace was that I spent my life among the elites. They treated me like a child, but simply being in their presence taught me how to move and speak like them. I would have to rely on that and hope my ability to mimic the rich and powerful was enough to prove to Lord Bessinger and Dame Farcile that I was a force to be reckoned with.

"The sun is setting," Ewig said, as we looked out over the looming horizon. The glistening armor of the army had been replaced with their tents that dotted the clearing on the horizon, creating a jagged silhouette reminiscent of sharp fangs. "They will be here soon."

"Do you think we are ready?" I asked as I tried desperately to keep my voice from quaking.

"Absolutely not," he said. "This is the finest fighting force this world has ever seen, and I say that acknowledging that we fought off the gods with one a century ago."

"These ones are better?"

Ewig scoffed. "The humans we fought with were a motley crew, held together by sheer heart and grit—two things these soldiers do not have— but ferocious training has taken its place, and dogmatic, zealous loyalty has been beaten into their bones."

"I'm scared," I said, pressing my stomach to hold in the butterflies that fluttered inside of it.

"So am I. My last hundred years have been spent trying to keep the eyes of the capitol off me, for fear of this exact eventuality. Only one thing could make it worse."

My eyes tracked down to the square, where two golden figures marched toward us. "What's that?"

"If my sister showed up in the sky to command her army personally."

"Is she really that ferocious?"

"Worse. However ferocious you fear her being, double it, and then triple that." Ewig's eyes found the two figures that moved toward us. "They are coming. I should make a show of it."

"I will see you back there."

"You'll do fine," he said. "I have faith in you."

Ewig extended his wings and flew high into the air, until his shadow blotted out the rising moon and made an incredible silhouette against it. Then, he dipped down again with a loud screech, and disappeared behind the volcano, where he would perch against the edge of the dining cave, blocking any egress, and allowing for us to watch out for any armed guards who might make a surprise attack.

I stepped out of the cave and held myself as high as I could as Lord Bessinger and Dame Farcile made their way up the narrow path toward me. He was wider than was comfortable to navigate the path, and his armor made it even bulkier. As he moved, he tripped and stumbled several times, which was comically hilarious, especially given our last encounter.

Part of me hoped he would trip and fall down the mountain. Dame Farcile seemed like an easier person to negotiate with than the gruff bear of a man who ran the emperor's army. However, much to my chagrin, Lord Bessinger successfully made it to the cliffs, and was able to climb them even with what must have easily been fifty pounds of plate armor, if not more.

By the time he reached the landing, his plate mail was dusty and scuffed. He had dents in his perfect gold. That was the problem with gold. It was quite beautiful, but overly malleable as well. It didn't take a beating well.

"You look a fright, commanders," I said to Lord Bessinger as he stood at attention. "Trouble finding the place?"

"It is not the finding which was troublesome, but the getting to it. I will admit, I thought you soft when we met, but anyone who could traverse this path and willingly face their death has more mettle than I gave them credit for."

I smirked. "Why, General, is that a compliment?"

"You should savor it," Dame Farcile said. "They don't come often."

"Then I will tuck it in my pocket, for use in the darkest moments, when I need it most." I turned to the cave. "Please follow me, the others are waiting."

I placed my hands in front of myself, pressed together in prayer, like I had seen Sister Milka do so many times, and took slow, shallow steps to help keep my balance in the high heels Mari insisted I wear. Even with them, I still barely reached Lord Bessinger's chest.

"Where is the dragon lord?" Dame Farcile asked.

"He will attend to you presently in the dining area," I said, stepping into the clearing where Ewig kept his fire burning. "He is most excited about it."

"You don't have to maintain the formality with us," Lord Bessinger said. "I know it might seem like we are some kind of fancy, but I would much rather share a beer with my men around a campfire than attend a gala in the capitol."

I nodded slowly. "I appreciate that courtesy, Commander."

However, I didn't let down my guard, or my pretenses, even slightly, as I walked. If anything,

I tightened my cheeks and pressed my shoulders back even more. I only thought everything was a test, and I would prove to him that we were more than the blasphemous heathens he thought us.

"This doesn't seem like a place fit for a lady," Dame Farcile said as we moved through the tunnel toward the dining area. "You really lived here?"

"For a little while," I replied. "I don't know how much you know of my situation, but I was only here, oh, less than a week before Leyhan found me, and we returned to the village with the others."

"We heard that these girls tried to kill poor Leyhan, and they murdered another man. Is that true?"

"It seems you have read the reports," I said to Lord Bessinger. "I cannot speak to the veracity of their claims, or the honesty of them, for fear of implicating my sisters."

"You must know how serious a crime that is," Lord Bessinger said. "To take the life of one of the emperor's subjects is tantamount to murdering the emperor himself."

I shouldn't have taken the bait, but it was such tasty bait. "And tell me, Commander, how many times have you murdered the emperor then, in your battles?"

He grumbled, "War is not the same."

"We are not at war, are we, Commander?" I asked.

"No, of course not."

"But you threatened my beloved. Is that not the same as threatening the emperor? Where do you draw the line?" I didn't let him speak when he opened his mouth. "Pardon me, where are my manners? Perhaps we should hold this conversation until after dinner."

"Yes," he grumbled again. "That might be best."

I continued on through the cavern, until it broke into the dining area. Half of the girls were seated at the table, with the other half busy bustling between the table, placing utensils and food on it. Behind them, Ewig sat, taking up the whole of the cave entrance, his head seated at the head of the table.

"Welcome to our humble home," Lord Ewig growled when his eyes found us. "We are looking forward to eating you." He smirked. "Sorry, I meant eating with you. Though, I suppose we'll have to see how the night goes as to which is more accurate by the end."

Chapter 26

Lord Bessinger was a surprisingly polite house guest and interesting conversationalist. He regaled us with tales of his battles, and the many things he'd seen across the world. He told stories about his greatest victories and most crushing defeats, with Dame Farcile seemingly there to echo his sentiments and confirm his grandiose tales. By the time we reached the main course, even I had been charmed by the old blowhard.

"And tell me," Ewig said as he nibbled on a hunk of boar Renata had caught earlier in the day. He seemed to be the only one unimpressed by Lord Bessinger's stories. "As the most accomplished commander in the emperor's army, why would they send you to this little corner of the world? There must be other matters that need attending than the misanthropes of a small little city at the end of the world."

The smile went from his face. "I don't think that is polite dinner conversation, so I have steered clear of it."

"So that you can drop the hammer during dessert?" Ewig asked. "How considerate of you."

"I have seen you peer out the cave and off into the distance several times during this dinner, so you must know that we, out of deference to your glory, dragon lord," Dame

Farcile said, "have not sent our soldiers into your sacred forest."

"I did notice that," Ewig replied. "Had you, I would have burnt you to a crisp where you stood."

"Another reason why we didn't," Lord Bessinger said. "However, the main reason we did so was out of respect for you. As you know, your sister honors respect above all things."

"Yes. I have always thought it a weird hill to die on," Ewig said. "Love, kindness, empathy. These are all better things to honor above all things."

Dame Farcile chuckled. "But, you see, respect contains all those things. If we respect your customs and traditions, then we show you kindness. If we respect your struggle, then we show empathy. If we work to respect your path, then we show love." Dame Farcile wiped her mouth. "So, your sister does honor those things."

"Your logic is infallible," Ewig growled.

"It is because of respect that we are here. Your blatant disregard for the rules places us in a tough spot. You are one of the dragon lords, so she fears your slight will embolden others to act against the crown, splintering the tenuous alliances that keep our world at peace."

"Peace is a funny thing," I said, "since you have spoken of so many of your battles. I would have thought a world at peace wouldn't have such need for bloody war."

"We are the hammer of the empire," Dame Farcile said. "Our job is to be the last line of defense, stamping out the embers of rebellion before they turn into a blaze. Just as a firefighter must use every means necessary to keep a fire at bay, from a boot to a bucket, so must the empire. We hope to solve our problems with the carrot, but sometimes, unfortunately, the emperor must rely on the stick. We are the stick."

"I thought you were the boot," Renata said, bitterness dripping from her mouth. "That's a better metaphor. Sticks burn after all, don't you know?"

"I don't know why you shear venom on us," Lord Bessinger said.

"Because you would have us die," Mari said. "And before you disagree, let me remind you that those sacrifices Ewig saved are seated around this table. We are the result of his defiance."

"Not all of them are here though, are they?" Dame Farcile said. "Some escaped some time ago, did they not?"

"It was nasty business," Ewig said.

"Yes," Lord Bessinger said. "Freja and Thersa said as much when they were arrested."

Renata slammed her hand on the table. "If you did anything to them—"

"Careful," Dame Farcile said. "We are not the enemy here."

"No offense," I said. "But if you are saying we deserved to die, that our crime is being alive and Ewig's crime is keeping us that way, and if you have imprisoned our sisters, then you are very much the enemy."

"Now, I hope that's not true," Lord Bessinger said. "If I thought we were enemies, then we would have to attack you with every bit of our might, which I assure you is substantial."

"We took the cedars for their protection," Dame Farcile said with pomp and authority. "Word circulated around the kingdom that a dragon lord was letting cedars live, and it started to foment all sorts of uncomfortable ideas around the empire. In some towns, I'm sorry to say, your sisters were tried as witches, and hung. Not every town is as tolerant as Yesiburgh. And so, we took them into our protection, and put them under Qyghem's care."

No. It couldn't be. Our sisters were dead?

"How many were slaughtered?" Ewig asked, anger and fire on his breath.

"Three, before we reached them, and another five were wounded. They have since recovered," Dame Farcile said. "Except for the three that died, of course."

"A pity, that," Lord Bessinger said. "Which is why we came here today. This insurrection cannot stand. The people will not stand for it."

"Insurrection?" I shouted, standing. "We are just trying to stay alive."

Lord Bessinger threw down his napkin and stood as well. "I can see this is getting contentious, so I will deliver what I was brought here to say." He cleared his throat. "We have orders to arrest all of the cedars in this town, and bring you, Ewig, to trial for sedition against the crown."

"Ha!" Ewig said. "Good luck."

"This is not a joke," Dame Farcile said, standing with her Lord. "If you do not comply, we will raze the town, the forest, and everything else for miles, until there is nothing left of this area but a charred bit of land."

Ewig shot a stream of fire between both the bodies of the soldiers. "Get out and tell your emperor and my sister we are not scared of them."

Lord Bessinger sighed. "We feared this would happen. Your sister hoped you would see reason. Perhaps you will still before the end."

"I will kill you now!" Ewig said.

"I wouldn't recommend it," Lord Bessinger said with a smile. "If I do not return within the hour, my men have orders to attack with extreme prejudice, leaving none alive."

"I will protect them with my life!" Ewig growled.

"And you might do an admirable job, dragon lord," Dame Farcile said. "But can you protect them all? Can you save every life?"

"Think about it." Lord Bessinger took his helmet from the table. "You have 24 hours to present yourself at our camp before we start a war that will lead to incalculable bloodshed and make you an enemy of the empire."

There was a long moment of silence when Ewig stared daggers at Lord Bessinger. Unlike in town, the commander didn't break, or blink. He must have summoned all his strength for this meeting. After what felt like hours, Ewig finally broke his gaze.

"Get out of my sight," Ewig growled. "NOW!"

With that, Lord Bessinger turned on his heels toward the exit. "It really was a lovely meal...until the end that is."

I walked toward them. "Let me see you out."

"We can find our way," he said.

"Oh, I insist."

He placed his hand in front of himself. "Lead the way."

Chapter 27

I kept silent up the stairs, and across the rope bridge toward Ewig's lair, and the front entrance to the caves. I didn't know what I was supposed to say, but as the self-appointed leader, and group appointed speaker for the cedars, I knew I was supposed to say something, but the words didn't come to me until we reached Ewig's room.

"I'm sorry that this devolved into such a—an unpleasant situation," Dame Farcile said.

I spun on my heels toward them. "And what did you think would happen when you told all of my sisters they were under arrest? Did you think they would go willingly?"

"It's for your own good," Lord Bessinger said. "There is already talk of rounding you up and feeding you to Ramidion herself. If you come with us, you will be safe."

"And in prison, for the crime of existing," I replied. "How is that fair?"

Dame Farcile shook her head. "It is not fair. None of this is fair, but it is the way it is."

"I am not swayed by what is supposed to be, only what should be. I have not studied the original charter since my early days at school, but my gut says that Ewig is right, there is no law that says he must eat us."

"That doesn't matter. It is how these things are done."

My eyes narrowed. "And you know that for sure? You have spoken to the other dragon lords, and they all devour their sacrifices?"

"Every one of them confirmed as such, and our soldiers checked their caves, and found no dwellings for them. What do you think we have been doing for the past year, since we heard of your treason?"

"Then they are every bit the monsters they appear in the storybooks."

"Watch it," Lord Bessinger said. "You know you are not allowed to speak ill of the dragon lords."

"We could not speak ill of the gods, either, if I remember correctly. I thought the dragons were supposed to usher in a new age of freedom, and yet, I see nothing but new rules supplanting the others, but rules all the same, as vicious and cruel as any other."

"The gods were capricious and mercurial," Lord Bessinger said. "They changed their rules on a dime and enjoyed when people fell ill of them. Ramidion brought structure to the world, consistency, and Lord Ewig has run afoul of it, throwing our whole set of laws into question."

"If our laws can be undone by kindness, then perhaps they should be reevaluated."

"That is not for us to decide," Dame Farcile said. "Ours is only to follow those rules."

I stepped forward. "I walked into the dragon's den for your rules. I believed in them so completely, I was willing to die for them, and now you tell me I should be arrested for having the gall to live in defiance of your death sentence. Tell me, General, what did I do that was so bad it warranted death?"

"You lived," Dame Farcile said. "It is a great honor to be chosen to sacrifice yourself to the dragon lord, and you besmirched it."

"If it is such an honor, then why do none volunteer for it?" My eyes filled with tears. "Why in a hundred years has no one offered to sacrifice themselves in place of us, if it is such a great honor?"

Dame Farcile's eyes dropped. "I—that is not how it's done."

I turned my attention to Lord Bessinger. "I plan on returning to town tomorrow and looking through the charter. Afterwards, I wish to entreat with you once again, on behalf of the others. Would that be acceptable to you?"

Lord Bessinger nodded. "You can do what you wish with the next 24 hours, but once the sun falls below the horizon tomorrow, that time will be over, and we will take you by force."

"Understood," I said. "And what of Leyhan?"

"He has been charged with inciting an insurrection. His fate is out of our hands."

"He was only trying to help us!" I shouted. "He's not a traitor. He's just a foolish boy, in love."

"So are most criminals," Lord Bessinger said. "I have slaughtered more children who loved their country enough to take up arms against me to know that, if you are old enough to swing a sword, you are old enough to be a threat."

I dropped my head. "Is there nothing I can do to earn his freedom?"

"Come to see me tomorrow, when the sun is at its peak, and we will discuss it further. For now, I really must go, lest our soldiers grow antsy in my absence and strike your city."

I nodded. "Of course. I will see you tomorrow, then."

Lord Bessinger placed his helmet on. "I look forward to it."

"That makes one of us." I pointed to the entrance of the cave. "I believe you can find your way from here. If you'll excuse me, I have much to discuss with my people."

Chapter 28

The air left my lungs, and I dropped to the ground the moment that Lord Bessinger and Dame Farcile were out of sight. I heaved loudly into the ground as I tried to regain my breath and my energy. I tried to push myself back to stand, but my legs were wobbly and uneasy, like gelatin.

"How did it—oh my lord!" Mari rushed toward me, as the others hurried along. "What did they do to you?"

"No—noth—nothing," I finally spat out. "I just—" I pressed my hand to my chest. "Lost my—breath."

Mari knelt beside me and rubbed my back. "The vapors, it would seem. They can be aggravated by stressful situations, like these."

The air finally returned to my lungs as my heart stopped slamming into my chest. I rocked myself to sitting and laid my head in my hands. "How did all this happen?"

"It happened because we dared to live," Fadia said. "The minute that we let those girls leave—" She turned to Renata. "I told you it would cause problems."

"And what were we supposed to do?" Renata replied. "We aren't a prison, and I wasn't about to kill them all. I'm not a monster."

"Not to them, no," Mari muttered. "Just to my brother."

It was low enough only I heard, but it seemed like Renata caught the gist anyway.

"What are you mumbling about, Mari? Did you have something to say?"

She shook her head. "It's nothing."

"It's not nothing. We're all screwed here, and if you think it's my fault, I want to hear it." She spun to the others. "In fact, show of hands. How many of you think this is all my fault?" No hands raised into the air. "See?"

"It's not your fault," Nur said. "And even if it was, it doesn't help us now. You heard Lord Bessinger. He's here to arrest all of us."

"Does that mean me?" Thorna said. "And Bella, too?"

I nodded. "I think so."

"Well, that is shitty!" Bella said. "I didn't even do anything!"

"Language!" her mother screamed.

"Shitty," her brother repeated with a laugh.

"Now look what you've done," her mother growled as she rushed him into the next room. "We don't use that kind of language."

"Oh please," Thorna said. "If this situation doesn't warrant foul language, what does? We didn't do anything wrong. We're not even supposed to get sacrificed for years. Why are we in this?"

"Because I highly doubt Ewig will eat you any more than he devoured us."

"She's right." The cave shook as Ewig ambled inside. "They will bring you to live out your remaining years in a prison until they decide where to sacrifice you to another one of the dragon lords."

"That's not fair!" Thorna shouted. "I'm finally free. Why can't they just let me go?"

I looked around the room. "I think that's the prevailing sentiment around here with all of us."

"So, what are we going to do about it?" Ewig asked. "Any ideas?"

"I am going to City Hall tomorrow to get a look at our copy of the original charter." Every city has a copy of the Black Charter, transcribed by monks from the original, signed by Emperor Paraphal I, great grandfather of our current emperor, and Ramidion, then countersigned by each dragon lord when they chose a territory. "Then, I'm going to talk with Lord Bessinger at his camp and see if we can come to terms."

"That's a waste of time," Thorna said. "That man will not bend for anything."

"But maybe it's a good idea," Renata said. "We said we needed a distraction to escape, and this might be a good one. When are you supposed to meet with him?"

"High noon, thereabouts," I said.

"That gives us until then to get ready to leave, and then—" She turned to Ewig. "How long will it take to carry us across the river?"

"I can't take all of you at once, I don't think, even though you are very small things." He thought. "I've made the trip in half an hour before."

"Wait," I said. "If we leave, then we condemn the town to death."

"I don't believe that," Ewig said. "If we escape without their knowledge, then we are traitors to the crown, not them. It might even make it easier if we simply extricate ourselves from the situation."

"And what if they burn them anyway?" I asked.

"Then they probably would have done it no matter what we did," Mari said. "And us giving up won't help anyway."

"How many trips would it take?" Renata asked.

"I think two," Ewig said. "Though it might take me a little longer while weighed down."

"Then you can take one group across, and come back in an hour, and then the rest of us will go."

"What about my daughter?" my mother asked.

"It's okay," I said. "I will gladly buy time for you to get away."

"Well, I'm not going without you," my mother said.

"Great," Renata replied. "Then we have our first volunteer for the second trip." She looked around the room. "Bella, her family, and Thorna should go first, since they're the smallest." She turned back to Ewig. "How many more can you take?"

"I can take two more, maybe three if they are small."

"That leaves me out," said Nur.

"No," I said. "You are older, and so is Fadia. You need to go first."

"We're old," Fadia said. "But we're hearty."

"It's okay," Mari said. "I'll stay. Somebody will have to speak for Renata if she is captured, and who better than the sister of the man she murdered?"

"Thanks," Renata replied, turning to Selma. "That means you."

Selma shook her head. "I'm not going anywhere without Mari. Not again."

Mari grabbed her face. "It's okay. We'll find each other again. I couldn't live with myself if I knew you were in danger in front of me."

Selma started to cry, pulled Mari close, and kissed her. It was a long kiss, longer than any of us were comfortable with. Everyone knew they were together for a time, and their different stances on returning to town drew them apart.

Now, it seemed that the intensity of this situation pulled them back together again.

"I love you," Selma said, finally breaking their kiss.

"I love you, too," Mari said. "Don't die, okay?"

"You either."

"Silly girl. I'm going to be right behind you."

"Still, we were apart for a year, and I don't want to be without you for another moment."

"Okay, gross," I said. "Cute, but gross. Take it outside or something."

"Agreed," Renata said. "So that's two groups. Mari, Gilda, Odine, and I will stay behind. You'll take the others, and the supplies across the—"
Ewig tilted his head. "What?"

"I can't take all of them and the supplies. You are lighter, so you'll have to bring them with you."

"And if we get caught?" Renata said. "They'll be trapped without anything."

"Then have one of them stay."

"We can't do that," I replied.

"Then you are at an impasse," Ewig said. "I'm a dragon, not a wagon."

"Fine," Renata said in a huff. "We'll bring the supplies with us. It will give us longer to gather anyway."

"Maybe we can let some of them go tonight," I said. "Save us the—"

"No," Renata interrupted me. "I need every one of them to gather as much as possible. We depleted a lot of our resources on that dinner. It will take hours to gather them all up again, and then pack them."

"Then why are we standing around here?" Mari said. "Let's get started."

Chapter 29

Renata led the group of us down the path, stopping every few minutes to clear a trap, or sidestep a snare. She and Ewig set up a series of barbs and spikes that worked with the rocks he laid down to impede an army from attacking us. The serpentine path around the rocks looked clear when looking up from the bottom of the path but looking down from the caves the deadly traps were clearly seen. She had people lay planks down so they would fall into them as she brushed past them.

When we finally got down to the bottom, she gathered us in a huddle. "Okay, split off into teams of two. Gather as much as you can, and when you're done, head back up to the cave. It takes an hour to get up and another to get back down, and we need each of you to make two trips, so don't dawdle." She pointed at Fadia. "Once you're paired off, Fadia will show you where to forage for berries, and put you to work clearing out her garden." She turned to me. "Meanwhile, we need to find some meat."

"Me?" I said. "Why me?"

"Because you're the only one who has actually snared a trap, and who I can trust to follow my instructions without getting themselves killed."

I nodded and followed Renata to the trunk where she kept her weapons. She handed me a bow and a machete, along with a quiver of arrows, and finally, two fishing poles.

"Don't worry. I'm not going to make you fish. You are dreadful at it. You can set traps while I do, though, and when I have a basket ready, you can bring it back."

"That sounds good to me," I said.

It took an hour to get to the lake, and an hour back, which meant we were cutting it close with even one trip, but we would be on the move after we landed on the other side of the lake, with little time left to hunt for food, so we had to try as best we could to gather meat for the journey. The more we brought with us, the more space we could put between us and the army.

"I just want you to know, I think this is a stupid plan, but false hope is better than no hope at all, right?"

"I guess so." I followed her over a downed branch. "Is that why you wanted to bring me with you, so you could be honest with me?"

She nodded. "You always were the only one I could talk freely to, at least after Freja left."

"Are you scared for her?"

She laughed, but I heard the hesitation in it. "I'm more scared for the army. She is nobody to be trifled with."

"I thought we weren't going to lie to each other," I said. "Or are you lying to yourself?"

"Of course I am," she replied. "How else could I keep going if I wasn't lying to myself?"

I knelt and set a trap, before moving along with her. We continued at that pace, stopping every hundred paces to lay another trap, until we reached the lake, and she cast both fishing lines into the water.

"Do you really think there's something out there?" I asked. "Across the lake?"

"Something, yes, or at least there was," she replied. "My great-grandparents came from over there, you know."

"Really?" I said. "I didn't know that."

"Word got to them that the dragon settled in the volcano, and they came to pay their respects. After all, the other dragons settled in populated areas filled with worshippers, and not in the middle of a forgotten forest. Many came to pay their respects, and some never left. That's the story of this place, though, right? Pilgrims came to worship at the great dragon's feet, to catch a glimpse of him, back before he became a hermit, and they built Yesiburgh on the grounds below his cave."

"Do you know where beyond the lake they came from?" I asked.

She shook her head. "No idea. I just know there's something out there, somewhere, and maybe we can start a new life there."

I chuckled. "I thought we weren't going to lie to each other."

"What do you want me to say? That we're going to die in a forced labor camp?"

I shook my head. "I won't let that happen."

She eyes me tightly. "No, you have a plan, don't you?"

It wasn't much of a plan, but I formed something while I was walking, but I feared telling Renata, in case she told the others. Still, I couldn't leave without telling somebody, because they had to make sure my mother got to safety.

"I'm going to try to offer myself, instead of all of you," I said. "If they can take me freely without bloodshed, then maybe that is a calculus they can live with."

"Yeah, I thought you would do some stupid thing like that."

I nodded. "It's pretty stupid, but I'm a Councilwoman, and I'm the last sacrifice. Maybe they can use me as an example. I can be their totem, especially if you are going out beyond the lake." I cleared my throat. "Besides, I could never live without Leyhan."

"You would be surprised what you can live without," she said. "Still, I'm not going to stop you, but Ewig might."

"No, he will be distracted trying to save you. That's the beauty of it all. By the time he finds out, the deal will be struck."

She reeled in one of her poles and cast it out again. "Personally, I think you should let them raze the whole town. Screw them all."

"I know you feel that way, and you know I don't."

"What if they don't accept?" she asked, looking out to the water. "What if they say all of us, or they raze the town?"

"Then you'll be gone," I said. "And I won't have much of a choice."

"You can tell them where we're going. We'll be in unsettled territory by then, and they'll have to spend days fighting through thick brush to get to us. I like our odds."

"I have no idea where you're going, and I don't want to know. I just know you'll be across the water, safe from the emperor and the dragon lords."

"Nowhere is truly safe from them," she said. "You know that. We'll be running for the rest of our lives, however long they might be."

"Not if I can help it."

Except, I wasn't sure I could. I had to try, though.

Chapter 30

We managed three trips back and forth to the lake by the time morning came but couldn't get in a fourth. I made one by myself with a bucket of fish, stopping to check the traps along the way and finding two voles and a rabbit snagged up in them. My heart still broke for them, but my focus on saving the other people in our camp tamped the ache of their deaths into a dull twinge.

Renata stayed at the lake to continue fishing and was able to fill another bucket and a half by the time I returned. By that time, we could see the haze of morning start to creep into the sky, and she knew it was time to return to the cave. She took one bucket, and I took another, filling up the half empty one with another vole, a chipmunk, and two squirrels.

"You really are a natural at this," Renata said, pulling the last squirrel from its noose.

"That's nothing to be proud of," I grumbled as she placed it into her bucket.

"You're helping to save all those people with this food," she replied, standing and grabbing the bucket. "You should be very proud. It's the circle of life."

"Yes, I think you said that to me once, right before you tried to kill my boyfriend."

"That's not fair." Renata continued past me toward the cave. "You act like they happened back-to-back, but the way I remember it we went trapping, then we found your boyfriend. Then, I tried to kill him much later."

"Yes, and you tricked him into carrying a doe back to the caves, and then ambushed him after he was of no use to you. I remember the chain of events."

"You seem more bitter about this than he does, honestly."

"He's a better person than me, and he knows how much you all mean to me. We're a package deal, you cedars and me, and he accepts the package, even if he doesn't love every part of it."

"That's true love if there ever was one. I could never accept people for who they were, it turns out. Freja always said that's why I liked the solitude of the woods."

"Can I make a confession to you?" I asked, weirdly worried she would judge me, even though I swore up and down that I didn't care what she thought about me. "Without you judging me?"

"I think we're long past judgement," she said. "So yes, yes you can."

"A part of me, a small part, is really excited to get to that prison, and see Freja again. I miss her terribly."

She smiled. "Why would I judge you for that? Freja is amazing, and if you weren't excited to see her, that's when I would think there was something wrong with you." She sighed. "How she looked at me, after, well, you know, it broke my heart to know I broke hers."

"How do you think they caught her?"

"She blabbed, for sure," Renata said. "She has a big mouth and always trusted people more than she should. It was her worst flaw, and her best." She looked over at me. "She's like you in that way."

"Was that another compliment?" I asked. "Are you feeling okay?"

"Of course not," she replied. "We're about to flee the only place I ever felt safe, and we're leaving the other girls in a work camp to have gods know what done to them."

"They won't be alone. I'll be there, too."

She brushed past a low branch. I recognized it enough to know we were getting close to the volcano. The verve was too thick to find our bearings, but the trees were distinct enough that we could find our way through the thicket.

"Is that supposed to make me feel better?" Renata asked. "Because feeding you to the wolves so we can escape doesn't leave a good feeling in my stomach."

"It doesn't leave one in mine, either, but if you all are able to get away, then it will be worth it."

"Have you thought about where Ewig is going to hide? He's a massive dragon."

I hadn't, in fact, thought about that. The cedars could disburse if necessary, or blend into the trees, but Ewig was an enormous dragon who stood taller than all but the tallest trees in the forest.

"Honestly, that's not my problem," I said. "I can buy you all time to escape, but what you do with it—well, I have to think of my safety, and Leyhan's. I trust you to figure it out."

"I don't know how much you should trust my instincts. They are the same ones that slayed Mari's brother and tried to kill Leyhan."

"Yeah, but they were also the ones who led us in a plan to escape when the army descended upon us."

"So, at best it's a wash." She sighed. "I fear we wouldn't be in this position without me."

"It wasn't you," I replied. "It wasn't any of us. Or maybe, it was all of us. This is not about your transgressions, or mine. It's about a stupid system that despises any deviation from their rules. We all screwed up by having the audacity to be alive right now, instead of digesting in the belly of a dragon." The trees broke and I saw the path up to the caves in front of us. "I'm not saying you didn't screw up, because you did, but they would have come for us eventually."

"Yeah," Renata said, sadly. "Maybe, but they wouldn't have left without what I did, and then— who knows what would have happened?"

"Leyhan would have still come for me, and I wouldn't have let you kill him, and if you let

Mari's brother go, he would have just told everyone. This was inevitable."

"Then I killed that poor boy for nothing."

"Yeah," I said. "And you have to live with that for the rest of your life, but you're also trying to save all of us, so at least you're atoning for it."

"I'll never atone for that black mark on my soul," she said.

"Maybe not, but all you can do is try. That's all any of us can do."

Chapter 31

We waited at the bottom of the hill for the last of the cedars to finish with their gathering, and then followed the path up, reengaging the traps along the way, until we reached the cave opening at the sun crested over the horizon.

"I wish we had time to smoke these," Renata said as she laid the fish and meat out on the cooking table.

"It's unfortunate," Nur said. "But we will cook them and do our best to preserve them in the time we have left."

"I don't know how much time we'll have to hunt once we get into the woods," Renata said. "We need to put as much distance between us and the army as possible, which means marching straight through at least one night, if not more."

The group had done well. There was an assortment of berries, vegetables, and meat laid on the cooking table. Now, however, they looked tired enough to fall over where they stood.

"You should rest for a couple of hours, and then begin packing."

Selma shook her head. "We'll sleep in shifts. We don't have a moment to lose. The youngest and oldest among us can take the first sleeping shift, and the rest of us will get to packing."

"I'm not leaving this stove," Nur said.

"Come on, dear," Fadia said. "Selma is right. You look terrible. A little rest will do you good."

"I've become quite an adept cook," Selma said. "In your absence."

"She's right," Renata said.

The arguing continued, but I had other things to do. I would have the benefit of sleep later, maybe after I was shackled. Now, I needed to change back into proper clothes, and prepare to leave for city hall.

"Can I help you change?" my mother said as I walked out of the cave hall.

"You should get some rest. It's going to be a long trek."

"I can sleep later, once Ewig has gone and before he returns."

"That's not much time. You'll need more than an hour of sleep to—"

"I am your mother," she snitted. "Not the other way around, and I would like to spend as much time with my daughter as I can before...well, let's just say I've already watched you walk into certain death once in my life, and I'm not excited to have you do it again."

"I'm not going to die, Mom," I said. "At least, I don't think I will."

"I don't trust Lord Bessinger as far as I can throw him, and that's not far. He's quite a large man, and that garish dress must weigh a ton."

I smiled. "Maybe two tons."

"Let me help you. Please. I know this is not easy for you."

I nodded and let my mother lead me to the baths, brush my hair, and dress me in a bright red velvet dress. It was quite a different experience from the last time I left her, when Sister Milka had overseen my dress, and we were inside our opulent house, surrounded by the grandest amenities in town.

"I don't know why you are doing this," my mother said as she combed a tangle out of my hair. "Haven't you done enough for them?"

"No, obviously somebody thinks not." I sighed. "I'm supposed to be dead right now, Mom. Just remember that. If you had your way—I would have been eaten by Ewig."

"Not my way!" she screeched. "I would never have wanted that for you."

"Every day I'm here is a blessing, a little miracle, like you said. If I die today, or tomorrow, or in twenty years, it's all bonus time, and with it, I want to spend every day trying to dismantle this horrible system that watches little girls sacrificed to dragons at the behest of powerful people."

"That's a noble goal, but it's also foolish."

I turned to her. "For the first time, my life is my own, and if I want to use it foolishly, please, just support me."

She nodded and choked back a tear.

When I was done dressing, my mother looked at me tenderly. "You really do look beautiful in that dress." She grabbed me by the cheeks. "Come back to me, okay?"

"I love you." I stared at her, stoically. "But you know that's not a promise I can make."

I slid her hands off my cheeks and walked out of the door. I heard her collapse onto the ground, and her sobs echoing through the cave while the others tried to sleep, but I couldn't bother myself with her feelings, and I couldn't spare them. I wouldn't let the last words I spoke to her be a lie.

Chapter 32

It pained me to leave my mother in such a frail state. I would have loved to comfort her, but there was no time for that. I had roughly twelve hours to find a way to save everyone, and the last thing I needed was my mother's frail mental state weighing on my mind.

When I returned to the dining cave, Selma and Mari were hard at work cooking as much meat as would fit over the steam, while Renata busied herself jarring berries into mason jars. I didn't know we even had mason jars, but I didn't have time to ask questions. I was due at city hall and wanted to be there when the doors opened.

I nodded my goodbyes to the cedars and continued up the stairs and over the rope bridge. I would have liked to spend more time with them, but if I opened my mouth, I feared I would spoil my plans, and ruin my nerve. I needed to keep my composure together for what would come next.

"How are they doing back there?" Ewig said as I entered his part of the cave. "I have heard them gossiping for hours."

"They are doing okay, given the circumstances," I replied. I had been so scared of the dragon lord for so long, but now, I saw a twinge of fear in him that made me pity him more than anything. "They are packing up for later. Are you sure you're up for this?"

"Absolutely not," Ewig said. "This sounds like a horrible plan. I've spent my life, at least the last century of it, holed up in this volcano. Do you know how hard it is to make a home in a volcano?"

"I have a bit of an idea, seeing as I was part of it for a time."

"There is not a suitable replacement for hundreds of miles in any direction, and even if there were, how long before they came for me? I'm not exactly inconspicuous."

"Then you fight and relocate."

He sighed. "There is nothing in this world I want less than a fight, and I certainly have no interest in relocating again and again. I am a creature of habit and being on the run breaks all of those habits." He scoffed. "Run. Dragons do not run from anything, and yet, here I am, planning to run."

"I'm going to fix this," I replied.

"No offense, Gilda, but you are a child, not only in my eyes, but in the eyes of the whole world. If I have not found a way out of this in a century, what hope do you have?"

"A fool's hope," I admitted. "But it is hope none the less."

He groaned. "I have been thinking this whole night that I should simply give myself to the guards and meet my sister face to face."

"That would be suicide and you know it."

"And would that be so bad if it were? If I could stop running this futile treadmill of—" He must have seen the horror that grew on my face. "Of course, you are too young to have these thoughts."

"No, I have them." I stepped closer to him. "I remember when I was walking up this path for the first time, to your lair, and I thought that perhaps it was for the best if I died, because I would not have to deal with the horrors of existence anymore. It's just—you are a dragon. You are supposed to be the strongest of us, and yet even you have these thoughts, and it gives me pause, that maybe I am not weak for thinking them."

"I have lived long, and learned many truths, some fleeting and others universal. One thing I know for sure is that we are not weak for existing, and we are not weak for welcoming the darkness into ourselves. This world is harsh, and cruel. There is great beauty in it, but also great horrors, and however we choose to get through the day, or choose to avoid that choice...neither makes us weak. Existence is insufferable."

I pursed my lips. "On that cheery note, I'm going to go and try to save all our lives right now."

"Do be careful," Ewig said. "Lord Bessinger is nobody to be trifled with."

"Neither am I."

I caught my reflection in Ewig's eye and could barely recognize myself. I stood tall and firm. My face was resolute and fierce. I looked, almost, like somebody who could carry the fate of everyone they loved on their shoulders, and not crumple under the pressure.

Chapter 33

I made my way down the narrow path barefoot. There was no way I would be able to keep my balance through the thin cracks in high heels. In fact, I decided I would not be putting on any shoes until I closed in on the camp later this morning.

"There she is!" the old woman who led the protests against us shouted to her group of grimy citizen-soldiers as they gathered around the entrance to City Hall. "The woman who would have our town razed to nothing."

"That's not what—listen. What is your name, ma'am?"

"Gertrude, of course. Friends call me Gerty, but you ain't one of those, heathen."

"Can you please move, Gertrude?" Her group blocked the stairs up to City Hall, and she was in the center of them, standing atop one of the pillars, proud and defiant. "I need to get inside."

"Of course you do, dragon meat!" She cackled. "But we're here to protect the peace and make sure you get what's coming to you."

"Sister Milka already said you couldn't hurt us without incurring the wrath of the dragon lords."

"Might be true, but it doesn't mean we have to help you, neither, dragon meat. We want the army to know that we don't approve of you all, and we don't support that traitor dragon lord you are betrothed."

I pressed my hands to my nose and turned away. Across the square, several dozen men and women passed. They each looked over at the crowd with a sense of disbelief, but they didn't come forward to help me.

Of course they wouldn't help me. What motivation would they have in sticking their own neck out for me?

"Hey!" I heard somebody with a thick accent shout in my direction. I turned, clenching my fist expecting a fight, but the tall, bushy bearded man growled straight past me toward the group. "You can't stop this woman from entering City Hall. It's her right."

"She's one of them cedars!" one of the men in the group shouted back.

"Oh, shut it, Tom," the bushy bearded man said. "She's a citizen of this town, and a councilwoman. Don't matter whether she should have been eaten by dragon lord Ewig or not, she's still a dang human being, and we should treat her with respect."

"If we do that," Gertrude said, "then the army might think we sympathize with her and slaughter us!"

"And why shouldn't we side with her?" a squat woman shouted, walking across the square toward us. "You don't have any sympathy for a girl who was supposed to be eaten by a dragon? What kind of heart do you have?"

"I am trying to look out for the whole town. My heart is big enough for all of you, even if you don't know it." She hopped down from her pillar toward us. "If we let her go on like nothing happened, it's the same as condoning her actions against the will of the whole army. Do you know what the army does to people who disagree with them?" She didn't wait for an answer. "They burn them alive, slaughter 'em all. Is that what you want?"

"If the only other option is to treat this girl like a criminal," the stout woman said, "then, yeah. I guess I do want that, but I don't think it's all black and white like that."

"Thank you both," I said, stepping forward. "But I don't want to cause any trouble for you."

"For us?" the bushy bearded man said. "How about the trouble we all caused you and your family, literally sentencing you to death?"

"That wasn't right, either," I said sadly. "But maybe they are right. Maybe I shouldn't even be here. Maybe I should just—I don't want you all to be in danger because of me."

"Gilda?" I turned to see Councilman Edward, the former mayor, walking toward me in his suit. "What's all this? Are you holding a rally?"

"She ain't with us," Gertrude growled. "We're here to stop her."

Councilman Edward sighed. "That was a joke, Gertrude. I'm very aware of what you're trying to do."

I stepped forward and leaned in toward the councilman. "Can you please just help me get inside? I just need one thing and then I'll be out of your hair forever. I promise."

"There's an entrance around back I used to use when I was mayor. I was supposed to relinquish the key but—" he patted the pocket of his jacket "—I couldn't part with it. Thought I might need it one day and seems like I was right."

I didn't like relying on the ex-mayor for a favor, but there was no other choice. I couldn't get past them on my own, and I couldn't ask the others to put themselves in danger for me.

"Thank you." Then I turned to the two people who came to my defense. "And thank you."

"Weren't nothing," the woman said. "Wish I could do more, like punch that old woman in the nose."

"I'd like to see you try it!" Gertrude shouted.

"Nobody's punching anyone in the nose here." I held up my hands. "Just calm down." When they were all quiet, I lowered my hands again. "I wish this town was more like the two of you, instead of them."

"They are," the bearded man said. "But you know how people are. The ones who bluster get all the attention, while most of us just want to keep our heads down." He sighed. "I wish I came when Leyhan called."

"Me too," the woman said. "He's a sweet boy, and I know how much he means to you."

"It's okay. Thank you for saying that."

"We should go," Councilman Edward said, grabbing my arm. "They aren't going to disband until you get out of their sight, and people are gonna be trying to get inside soon. I would rather not have any more people hate you for something you had no control over."

Chapter 34

"Thank you," I said, as Councilman Edward opened the back door of City Hall. It was an inconspicuous, brown door that led into an equally nondescript hallway. "I was planning on sitting outside until it opened. I didn't expect to get into a row with anyone."

"Well, tensions have been high since the military arrived and put up those stupid posters."

"Renata doesn't think this town is worth saving, but it's people like you who make me disagree with her."

He opened a door into an office suite and continued down a row of plush offices. "Well, I don't know about that. I was the only one who oversaw your sacrifice last year, and I believe I even tried to convict you for it when you came back."

"People can change. That is the beauty about them. They can grow and evolve."

Councilman Edward opened a door into the main hallway. I heard the protestors on the other side of the door and worked to prevent my body from seizing up in a combination of anger and fear.

"Where are you headed?" he asked.

"The archives. I need to see a copy of the Dragon Charter, the one that laid out the rules for the sacrifice. I'm trying to prove that whatever Ewig did wasn't against the law, and that we are his property to do what he wants with."

"Oof," Councilman Edwards said. "I'm not sure how to feel about you being property."

"As you made abundantly clear, a year ago you tried to have me killed. Property is a step up from that fate."

"Sure, but I'm not sure I like either fate, frankly. And this is the argument you're going to make to who, Lord Bessinger, to try and save your life? To say that you can't be tried for crimes because there were no crimes, and that Ewig is innocent because you are his property to do what he pleases with, even if he pleases to keep you alive?"

"It doesn't sound great coming from your mouth," I said. "But yes, essentially that is it. Perhaps he will see it in his benevolence to let us go from our bondage to him, eventually, but until then, I am indebted to him for my life, and my safety."

"Then, I guess I can show you the way. It was under my purview as mayor to review it every year. I used to have it committed mostly to memory, but after the election, a lot breezed out of my brain to make room for everything new."

He led me down the hallway, across from the City Council chamber where I had sat so many nights, and pushed the doors open on an enormous library that held records of everything from corn production to bank debt, and every transaction in our town's history.

"You'll appreciate this, or maybe you won't." He pulled out a small ledger from a shelf as we walked past it. "This is the ledger to prove that we followed all the procedures for each cedar. Lord Bessinger requested to review that personally. Of course everything was completely above board, at least for the past three sacrifices. I made sure of it myself."

"Except for the killing us part," I reminded him.

"Yes, of course not that part, but we had no idea he would keep you alive. It's been known for ages that dragons consume their sacrifices."

"The question is whether that is colloquial knowledge or written down in the rules somewhere."

We stopped in front of an enormous glass case. In front of us, under glass, was the original town charter laying on the right of the display, and the Black Charter on the other, written in gold leaf on a single sheet of black paper. Illustrations of fearsome dragons lined the margins, and the script was written with fancy flourishes on every line.

I bent over the case and read it eagerly.

"It is hereby decreed by his majesty, King Paraphal I, and Dragon Lord Ramidion, that on the solstice of every fifth year, a virginal maiden shall be given to each dragon lord, chosen from

*the town nearest its providence, to acknowledge
the good fortune of being under their protection,
and in acknowledgement of the blood they spilt in
ridding our world from the menace of the gods.
Said virgin will be considered to be the first
female child born after the previous sacrifice, and
said tradition shall continue in perpetuity, until
the end of time."*

Then, it was signed by Emperor Paraphal I, Ramidion, and Ewig.

Given, not sacrificed, or murdered, or burned, or any such word. The contract simply says given to the dragon lord, which meant Ewig was right. He could do whatever he wanted with us, including let us live.

"I think I just found our loophole." I turned to Councilman Edward. "I'm going to need that contract."

Chapter 35

Councilman Edward furrowed his brow. "I'm afraid I can't do that. Only the mayor and the head of the library can open this case, and we are neither."

I looked over at him, angrily. "You realize I have nothing to lose, right? I'm trying to be polite, but I could smash this case and take the stupid thing. Everybody wants me dead anyway."

He smirked and took a step forward. "You are a very small girl. Do you really think I couldn't hold you down if the situation called for it?"

I shook my head. "Of course not. You already sent me to my death, so I don't believe you have any morals at all, but I want to believe you are better than your darkest impulses, and if you have any desire for redemption, to atone for what you have done to my sisters and I, then here is the chance to exercise it. Instead of being our jailer, you could be our hero."

His face dropped. "Is that what you really think of me?"

"Yes, and that is why you helped me this morning, isn't it? Because you do not want to be the monster from our nightmares."

He turned away. He looked like he was about to cry. "Not only from your nightmares, but my own, too. The minute you returned from that volcano, hand in hand with Leyhan, it was like a grand illusion shattered in front of me, and I saw what I had become."

I stepped forward and touched his hands lightly. "That is why everyone is angry at us, I think. It has nothing to do with us, but because of what we represent to them." I sighed. "I will tell you a secret. I am going to turn myself in today and beg for my life. I am going to do it to save my sisters, yes, but also to save this town from a vicious fate, but I need that contract."

Tears fell down his face. "Why would you do that, after how we treated you?"

"Because there is good in this town. I have seen it, but more importantly, how you treat me is on your soul, and how I choose to treat you is marked on mine. I will not throw away anyone, for any reason. I know too well what that is like." I stepped back from him, dropping his hands. "Now, something tells me that the key to the back door wasn't the only thing you kept whcn you left your old post."

He pursed his lips and winced. "You know what will happen to me if I give this to you."

I shook my head. "No, I don't, and I don't because I am alive and should be dead. If my life demonstrates nothing else, it's an example that we never know what will happen, the impossible can happen, and that expectations don't have to match reality."

He didn't say anything else, just let out a long sigh and pulled the key out of his pocket. "This is actually a skeleton key. It opens any door in this building, including this one."

He placed the key into the lock and gave it a twist. The glass popped open, and I carefully picked the paper from it, careful to grab it only by the edges to preserve the delicate paper. When I had it in my hands, I carefully twisted the paper between my thumb and index finger until it was taut.

"What's the meaning of this?" I heard from the front of the room, as the head archivist, Mr. Twissle, a slender, balding man with thick glasses and a bushy salt and pepper mustache, came storming through the halls. "You do not have authority to be in here, missy."

"I am on the city council! That gives me every right—"

"You are a wanted fugitive now," Mr. Twissle said with a smug smirk.

I went on the attack, ready to defend myself, when Councilman Edward stepped in front of me. "It's okay, Frank. She's with me."

Mr. Twissle stopped abruptly, confused and shocked. "But I don't understand. You know you can't take that out of the building. It's against the rules."

"The rules went up in smoke a year ago," Councilman Edward said. "We've been lying to ourselves since then. And now we have the army at our doorstep, threatening to raze our whole village unless this girl and the other cedars give up and let themselves be arrested." He straightened his back. "That's not good enough for me. Councilwoman Gilda thinks this scroll can help plead her case, and thus, I allowed her to take it."

"On whose authority?" he asked.

"On Ewig's authority," I said with as much bravery as I could gather. "I speak for him on all matters in this town, and if he means anything to you still, then my words are his bond, and my actions his."

Mr. Twissle swished his lips from one side to the other as his eyes narrowed, sizing me up as his head cocked from one side to the other. Then, with a concerted nod, he turned away.

"Very well," he said. "If you are here on his authority, then I cannot stop you. I'm not sure I believe you are on his authority, but it is too early in the day for me to get into a big thing with you. However, if you are stopped, then I never saw you, and I certainly didn't let you go. Understood?"

"That goes double for me," Councilman Edward said.

"Understood," I said. "My lips are sealed."

Mr. Twissle stormed back to his desk and pulled out a long leather tube, before returning to me and slamming it into my palm. "And I definitely didn't give you this carrying tube to prevent it from being exposed to the elements."

Chapter 36

Councilman Edward opened the back door and I slid out of City Hall and around the side without notice. I stopped when I saw the protest, not because they had grown more threatening, but because a counterprotest started across the square. I saw Bernice's family, and the nice, bearded man from earlier, along with the stout woman. There were not as many of them as the protesters gathered on the steps of City Hall, but as I watched, a half dozen more people joined the others in the square.

I couldn't help but crack a smile. Leyhan was right. It took longer than we would have liked, but people were coming to defend us, and our honor. We weren't the pariahs we believed. I wished the other girls and their families could see the people gathered to fight for us.

Looking at them, my resolve grew even stronger to fight to protect them, however, I believed every word of what I said to Councilman Edward. It didn't matter how they felt about me, even if every one of them hated me with a passion. What mattered was how I dealt with them, and the actions I took to defend them. No matter how much they despised me, and no matter the vile things they spewed at me, even the worst of them deserved to live. If my time as a cedar taught me nothing else, it was that.

The army was stationed on the outskirts of town, and even if it took an hour to reach them, I had plenty of time to spare before the sun was high overhead, and I needed to use every moment of it to buy my sisters enough time to get away to safety.

While I waited, there was one person in town who knew more about the dragon lords than anyone, and I needed her opinion before meeting with Lord Bessinger.

Sister Milka lived in a small convent behind the church, with a small congregation of sisters. It was little more than a two-story house, but it was marked with the sigil of the Emperor, and the circular cross of the church, an endless cycle depicting the age of the world, bisected by a single horizontal line at the center of it to signify the connection between humanity and dragon kind. The line extended beyond the confines on each side of the circle to show how we broke the constraints of the gods by taking our destinies in our own hands.

I knocked on the wooden door, and a thin, tiny woman opened it. I knew her as Sister Gwendolyn, who led prayers every week, and taught at the school in the afternoons.

She was surprised to see me, and it read all over her face. "Councilwoman Gilda. This is a shock. I didn't expect to see you here today of all days."

I nodded. "Yes, I know that my appearance here is sudden, but I have an urgent need to speak with Sister Milka."

She placed her hands on her chest. "Bless your heart. I know she was very important to you, and you want to say your goodbyes to her. Let me show you to her room."

Of course she assumed I would give myself to the army. After all, I was trained to sacrifice myself for the greater good, and what was my life, all our lives, compared to the lives of the entire town? Still rude, though, even if she was right.

"Sister Milka," the nun said, knocking at a door at the end of the upstairs hallway. "You have a visitor."

"Go away," Sister Milka's grumpy voice growled. "I'm not taking visitors."

"Please," I said, stepping forward. "It is urgently important that I speak to you."

"Gilda?" The sound of a chair moving on hardwood preceded her opening her door to see me. "You look proper, for once."

"You always were a charmer, sister," I said. "I come on urgent city business and need to speak with you forthwith. May I come in?"

She moved aside and welcomed me into her room before turning to Sister Gwendolyn. "You may kindly go away, please. I am in need of solitude to counsel this cedar."

"Very well, sister." Her tone was biting, though her words were kind, as she turned and walked down the hallway.

Sister Milka's room was plain. A small, wire-framed bed rested against one wall, and against the other rested a wooden writing desk in front of a four-panel window that looked out to the church, and the square beyond it.

"To what do I owe the pleasure?" Sister Milka said.

"As you no doubt are aware, the army has demanded my arrest, and that of my sisters. We dined with Lord Bessinger last night, and he invited me to his tent at midday to discuss our terms for surrender." I held up the leather tube. "I have something I would like for you to look over and give your opinion on."

She lowered her eyes. "I don't know what good I can do. Since you returned from the caves, I have been a laughingstock."

I pulled the Black Charter out of the tube and unfurled it on the writing table. "Be that as it may, you still know more about the workings of the capitol, and the cedars, than anyone in town, and I am in need of your eyes to see if I have missed anything."

She stepped forward, hands on her mouth. "How on Earth did you get this?"

"That's not important. What is important is that I believe it says nothing about the dragon lords having to eat their sacrifices, just that we are to be given to them as tribute. Lord Bessinger believes it says differently, but this contract, to me at least, clearly states the truth. Can you please look at it, and give me your opinion as to whether my argument holds up to scrutiny?"

She sighed, opened a drawer underneath the contract, and pulled out a pair of reading glasses. "I'll do what I can. After all, if what you're saying is true, then I didn't waste the last fifty years of my life."

Chapter 37

Sister Milka stared at the contract for a long time, feeling the edges of it. "I have never seen this document outside of the glass case, you know?"

"But you're the one responsible for all the cedars. How is that possible?"

She looked over at me. "I wasn't important enough to touch it, no matter how much I asked, so, over time, I stopped asking." She felt the grooves of the uneven parchment. "It's quite a thing, isn't it?"

"That contract condemned me to death, so it doesn't have quite the reverence for me that it does to you."

She faked a smile. "Of course. What was I thinking?" She turned back to the document and scanned it closely. "It was quite an honor for a long time, you know? Being a cedar has fallen out of favor over the years, but when I started, the cedars were lauded, celebrated even, and they were happy to be chosen."

"I find that hard to believe. Fadia and Nur didn't seem to feel it was much of an honor."

She kept her head on the contract. "Time has a habit of dulling the truth, but Nur specifically was giddy over the idea of serving her community in such a manner. How many have a chance to make a real difference in their lives?"

"Except it wasn't a real difference, was it?"

"No, it wasn't, but we didn't know that. We were—all of us—duped." She stayed silent as she read the document again. "Well, I must say I believe your reading of this document is accurate. Nowhere does it say that you must be devoured, only that you must be freely given."

I paced the room. "Then how did that become the parlance of our time?"

"You don't know much about the first cedars, do you?" She sighed. "No, of course not. You were always a decent student, but history was never your subject, was it?"

"Hey! I memorized every cedar back to the beginning for you."

"Yes, but memorization isn't enjoyment, is it? It's not part of the curriculum to read about the first cedars, and you were never one to seek out knowledge for its own sake."

"Rude. Why is everyone being so rude today?"

She took off her glasses. "It's not your fault, dear. It's a failing of the school system. The origins of the cedars was a murky, mucky time with many shades of gray, and gray was never a good color on history, so it was paved over."

"And what happened with the first cedars?"

"Well, Yesiburgh didn't always have them, for one. Ewig was the last of the dragons to find a home, and then it took even longer for the town to develop around him. We were a hundred years into the age of dragon lords before the first edict came down, and we received our version of the Black Charter, signed by the emperor and Ramidion, and countersigned by Ewig himself." She pointed to the bottom of the contract, where I clearly saw Ewig's name in beautiful red script. "He really does have good penmanship for a dragon."

"Quite," I replied. "But what does this have to do with anything?"

"I'm getting there." She shook her head. "The impetuousness of youth."

"More like the impetuousness of that I only have until sundown to fix all of this. So, please, for the love of the dragon lords, get to the point."

"Fine, fine, fine. The point was that by the time we began our cedars, they were well established by the other kingdoms, and the army oversaw us for the first several decades, until we fell in line, and could be counted on to lead the ceremony without their oversight." She smirked. "That only happened when I came along, of course, and brought stability to the practice. Before then, this was a military hotbed."

"Don't expect me to thank you."

"Oh, I never expected thanks, and I didn't get it, either. Did you know there was quite a little rebellion before the first sacrifice? Citizens had no interest in forfeiting their daughters to the dragon lord. It wasn't until Yesibel stepped up and agreed to set an example that there was precedent. Though it was shaky, every five years we looked back to Yesibel's sacrifice and followed through with another of our own. That is why we call it Yesiburgh, incidentally."

"Did the military threaten to destroy the town if we didn't participate?"

"Of course." She pursed her lips. "And we were willing to go to war with the military, too, for the honor of our girls. You can see why they would keep that from the approved history books. We have always been a thorn in the side of the capitol. Too far out to rule properly, and too stubborn to stay in line for long. After all, what other kingdom under a dragon's rule has a democracy?"

"I don't—"

"None, dear. They are all ruled by facists. If you ask me, that was what truly drew them here, our wild streak. It was prompted by you, of course, but we have never been Emperor Paraphal's favorite people."

"That's a great story, I guess," I said. "But what of the contract? Do you think we have a case?"

She chortled to herself. "You don't understand what I said at all, do you? It doesn't matter what you bring to them. They have already made up their minds about us."

"I don't believe that."

"An adorable sentiment." Her lips turned up in a pained smile. "Unfortunately, that doesn't matter."

"I'm going to prove you wrong. Just watch."

"Nothing would make me happier, though it is a fool's errand." She carefully rolled up the parchment and delicately lowered it back into the leather tube. "I do wish you luck though. It is not fair that so much has been placed on your shoulders, but then, life is not fair, and Ramidion is certainly not, either."

"Thank you."

"Just think about this." She placed the tube in my hands. "Why would they set up camps if they were only here to capture you and flee? Doesn't that sound odd to you?"

"Umm...yes? I guess so. I never really thought about it."

"It sounds odd to me, too. Be careful out there. Something strange is afoot."

Chapter 38

I took the contract with me when I left Sister Milka, along with an unsettling feeling in my stomach from the story she told me. Could the army being here really be retaliation on a town that had always been rebellious? I doubted it, but Sister Milka was not one who told tall tales. She despised lying and even disliked fiction because it was one big lie that traveled from person to person, so I doubted she made any of it up, though her imagination might have been connecting dots that have no reason to be correlated.

No, just because she said it didn't mean I had to believe her ideas about why the army was here. They were not here to punish the town, just the cedars, and the dragon lord for going against their edicts. That made the most sense.

The path out of town was wide enough for two carts to pass each other, but not much more. A rickety wooden sign hung over the arc, welcoming all to Yesiburgh, and another marking that we had left hung on the other side. When I passed under it, my heart skipped a beat. I was sure I had left Yesiburgh for the last time, a town I had lived in all my life.

The woods thickened as I walked deeper through them, and I felt eyes following me, hot on my neck, as I stepped through the woods. The trees were thicker here than even on the other side of the volcano, and night seemed to fall as I traveled deeper into them. Only the occasional beam of light breaking through the tree line indicated that sun still shone through them.

Every so often, a branch would snap, or the brush would rustle, and I would jump at the perilous thought, hoping that whatever tracked me was a benevolent force and not a malicious one. I had enough of those in my life.

I was suddenly aware of my size, and how I had no weapons on me, save for a leather tube that wouldn't scare much that chose to attack me. Still, I continued stepping forward, one after another, as the dirt path grew into grass the further I walked from town. Carts rarely came through from other areas of the world. We were on the edge of the emperor's kingdom, which stretched from the lake behind Ewig's volcano, five thousand miles across to the other side of the world, and two thousand miles north and south, to the fringes of the planet. There were other kingdoms, but they were small and insignificant. The only reason they were not part of the emperor's empire was because he was uninterested in them. If he wanted them, they would be his in a fortnight. After all, he was the only one with dragons.

After two hours of walking, the trees broke into a large clearing, where the king's men had set up tents along the horizon. I didn't realize how large they were from the volcano, but the tallest of them were bigger than the church and the school in town and seemed to stretch a full city block.

Several soldiers in glimmering and glistening armor made their way across the tents, patrolling the grounds, while others sat around campfires, armorless, whittling, smoking from pipes, or any manner of recreational activity. It surprised me how casual they could be, when just yesterday they were in full battle regalia, threatening to raze the town to the ground.

I remembered what Sister Milka told me before I left her bedroom, and seeing it all, it seemed like they were here for a long stay, not just to arrest us and move on back to the capitol. No, this was an occupation. The thought of it sent my stomach into my knees.

"Can we help you, miss?" a gilded soldier said, walking up to me like I wasn't even a little bit of a threat to her.

"I'm Gilda." I said. "I am here to see your Lord Bessinger. He is expecting me."

She looked at me for a long moment. "Oh yeah. I remember you. The girl with the dragon. You're surrendering? How sad. Honestly, I was hoping you would put up a fight. I never fought a dragon before."

"Just because I don't come with my dragon, or weapons, do not think I will not put up a fight. I have no interest in going quietly into the night."

Her eyes narrowed. "Is that a threat? Because I have to cut you down if that was a threat."

I shook my head. "I mean you no harm. All I have is a simple leather tube, with a flimsy piece of parchment inside."

I held up the tube and she reached forward to take it. "I'll have to take that, after what you said."

"As long as it gets to Lord Bessinger safely, and me as well, then I have no problem with you taking it. However, as I said, neither of us are threats to you."

"No offense, miss, but just the fact you're still alive is a threat, if what I hear is to be believed."

"And what do you hear?" I stepped forward slowly. "I am a sixteen-year-old girl, with no armor or weapons. I am barely educated, and I have no army behind me. It seems comical that I could hurt you, doesn't it?"

She nodded. "Admittedly, yeah. It seems a little foolish, but that's what I was told."

I looked up into the sky. The sun was nearly overhead. It had taken me longer to get through the woods than I thought. "Can we continue this while we walk? Your Lord Bessinger really is expecting me, and he doesn't seem like the type that likes to be kept waiting."

Chapter 39

I couldn't help but still feel the heat from eyes boring into my back as we walked through the encampment. Every time I passed another group of soldiers, they sat at attention. Those that didn't recognize me were quickly filled in by those who did, and by the time I reached the red and yellow tent at the center of the encampment, the whole army was aflutter with whispers and activity.

"Wait here," the soldier said as she disappeared inside the tent.

As I waited, I watched the soldiers trying in subtle and blatant ways to point me out to their compatriots. I was an oddity, the girl who survived being sacrificed to a dragon, and everyone wanted to get a good look.

I couldn't have been much to look at, especially after being built up in the heads of the soldiers. I was short, and plump, though the lack of extra rations trimmed me down considerably in the past year, especially since I had exponentially increased my walking during that time. I held a lot of baby fat in my cheeks still, but the outline of my jaw and chin were certainly more visible now than they were in the past year.

As I watched the soldiers watch me, some leering, some dejected, and others amused, I felt suddenly self-conscious in a way that only the whispers of the villagers had made me before. I wanted badly to disappear into the nothing, but that was another girl's purview. I had to stay strong, and brave for my sisters, and for the whole town, but it was hard with the gawking gestures of the army soldiers.

"He'll see you now." The tent flap opened and mercifully my escort emerged just as I nearly reached my breaking point. "Go inside."

I passed the soldier and entered the tent. Red and yellow light bounced off the tent walls and caused a hazy glow inside, augmented by several torches placed around the room, and a lantern on Lord Bessinger's desk in the center of the room.

"Is this a joke?" Lord Bessinger growled as he pointed to the black contract that laid on his desk. "Tell me true."

I shook my head. "Of course not. I took it from city hall myself. It was under lock and key until I liberated it."

"Hrm, and I'm sure somebody can vouch for that."

I opened my mouth but thought better of it. I didn't want to implicate either of my co-conspirators, though unwilling ones, in my theft. "If one of your men visits city hall, I am sure it will not be there."

"And what's to stop you from stealing the original and replacing it with this forgery?"

"On my honor, that didn't happen," I said. "Firstly, I don't know where I would find black paper aside from Ramidion's personal collection. It is incredibly rare, and only the most royal decrees are written on it."

"You could have dyed it," Lord Bessinger said.

I stepped forward again. "I'm sorry to have caused you such consternation, but please, why are you so concerned that this is a forgery?"

He looked at me. "You really don't know?"

"On my life, which I value even more than my honor."

He stepped from around the table. "Because if that's the real Black Charter for Yesiburgh, then it has been altered from the original text, and the contract between your town and Lord Ewig is unlike any other in the empire."

"I don't understand," I said.

He spun back around. "This word 'given', on this paper. It is supposed to say 'sacrificed'. It has been altered from the original text."

"I see," I replied. "I thought it was odd that you were so adamant about us being sacrificed, so I looked up the charter, and when I found this irregularity, I brought it directly to you, posthaste."

He sat back down at his desk. "I have sent a soldier with a sample to our best alchemist to verify its origins, and age. We will soon see if you are a liar, or your whole town has been duped."

"How could this be the town's fault? If I have heard correctly, your men were here at the first cedar, and came back for decades to make sure we made the sacrament correctly every year. Is that not true?"

He cocked his head. "You are more learned than your age suggests. Yes, that is correct, but we would never have a need to look at the contract, unless something went wrong, which we didn't know about until right now."

"If this is a valid contract, then what does it mean?"

He growled. "It means somebody royally screwed up, and you might have been right all along."

The thought of it filled me with hope for a moment, but I had learned not to fill myself with hope. Men's words were also said with caveats, and while they spoke pleasant words, their truths came from the sides of their mouths.

"May I see Leyhan while we wait?" I asked.

"I already told you he is a prisoner of the state. As such, he has no right to have visitors, or see his loved ones."

"Oh please," I growled. "You only have him locked up because he tried to help us, and if we are to be free of our bondage, then you have no cause to hold him."

"That's cute," Lord Bessinger said.

"What is?" I asked.

"That you are naïve enough to believe I need a reason to do anything. The advantage of being in service to the emperor is that I have no need for such things as legal recourse."

The flap of the tent whooshed open, and the soldier walked in, followed by a careful man with calloused hands and stubble on his rough face.

"Speak, alchemist," Lord Bessinger growled.

The alchemist looked at the soldier, who nodded, and then to Lord Bessinger. He swallowed loudly before he spoke. "I have authenticated the blood, the ink, and the paper." He took another deep breath. "They all match both the time period, and the properties of their contemporaries."

"Are you sure about that?" Lord Bessinger asked.

"Absolutely, sir. We keep records of such things, and I cross referenced them twice to be sure."

Lord Bessinger looked as though all the wind had been knocked out of him. "Well, that complicates things."

Chapter 40

"It doesn't sound that complicated to me," I said to Lord Bessinger as he stood in front of me inside his oversized tent. "That contract seems to prove that we shouldn't be arrested for having the audacity to still be alive."

Lord Bessinger stroked his chin. "Yes, it would appear as such. And tell me dear, have you shared your findings with anyone?"

Ominous energy dripped from his mouth, compounding with each word, until by the last word I had been consumed with a cold shiver. I didn't want to get anyone in trouble, but something deep in my bones told me that if I didn't tell the truth, I was in immediate, mortal peril.

"Well, there was Sister Milka, who confirmed my suspicions, and Councilman Edward, who I consulted after I had possession of the contract. Oh, and the librarian, Mr. Twissle."

He furrowed his brow and shook his head slowly. "Well, that is a pity." He snapped his fingers, and two soldiers entered the room, towering over me, and casting a dark shadow as they loomed large overhead. "Take these two. Gag them and put them somewhere nobody would look for them."

"What?" the alchemist cried out. "No, please. I wouldn't say anything. I swear."

Lord Bessinger's eyes narrowed. "I simply can't take that chance."

I struggled against them, but the two firm hands that wrapped around me were strong, and their grip tight. The soldier picked me up with little effort, even with me kicking and squirming against him.

"You won't get away with this!" I screamed.

But Lord Bessinger looked uninterested in my commentary. He picked up the black paper and wrapped it back into the leather tube, before tipping his lantern into it, and throwing it in a metal wastepaper basket next to his desk.

"*What are you doing?*" I screamed. "You can't destroy that contr—"

"Poor girl." He walked toward me, slowly. The alchemist had already been taken away, kicking and screaming until he was out of sight, and his voice faded in the distant wind with every passing second. "You have no idea how this world works, do you?"

I stopped struggling against the soldier and allowed him to hold me tightly against his cold armor. I pulled my head tight to stare intently at Lord Bessinger.

"I'm starting to get an idea. I thought you were a man of honor, but I can see your true colors now."

He scoffed. "Honor is a luxury children maintain, and those who are naïve to the ways of the world. There was a time when I believed in such pedantic notions, but honor does not turn the world, not when it rewards dishonor above virtue."

He was nose-to-nose with me now, inching closer with every word from his mouth.

"So what now? You kill me as a warning to stay in line?"

He pushed back, standing broadly above me. "That is such a crass notion. Do you think so little of us?"

"On the contrary. I think much of you. I think you will do anything to maintain power, no matter how much is expected of you. So what will you do to me, then?"

He turned back to his desk. "You are highly prized by Ramidion, and thus you are an important bargaining chip for the emperor. You will be brought before him, just as soon as we are able to find the rest of your ilk and bring back Ramidion's prize."

"Ewig will never come before you. He is long gone."

"Yes, we noticed him taking a contingent of cedars across the lake early this morning."

My eyes went wide. "How can you—how did you—"

"What?" he replied. "Know that you would plan to run, even though I expressly told you that if you ran it would condemn Yesiburgh to burn?" He stepped forward. "Because you have no honor, just like me, and I know how people like me think. Tell me, what did you think you would get out of coming here today?”

“I don’t have to tell you anything.”

“You’re right,” he replied. “But if you don’t, then I have no reason to keep you around.” He snapped his finger. “Take her away.”

“No!” I shouted. “Please.”

“Then tell me the truth. We are long past games, girl.”

“I was planning to offer myself as a captive, in exchange for the freedom of the others. I thought that the contract, plus my willing servitude, would be enough to save the others, especially since it came without bloodshed.”

“But you did not expect me to burn your offer before you could make it, did you?”

I shook my head. “No, but then again, I thought you had honor. You have assuaged me of that notion most expertly since then.”

“And what makes you think that you could be a prize enough for a god?”

“I was the last cedar, and I speak for them on the city council. You do not need us all to make a point. You need a symbol, and I thought I would be symbol enough for you.”

He chuckled. “Why would I accept a symbol, when I could have you all?”

“Because you could leave without risking your troops.”

He smirked. "They are nothing to me but pieces on a chessboard. I have long since given up my personal attachments to my soldiers, just like you should to your precious cedars. It is the only way to do this work."

I didn't have a good answer. "Just please, don't hurt them. They've done nothing wrong. You've seen that yourself. They are nothing to you, both the town and the cedars. You could turn away and nothing would change for you. We are small, and benign. We have no trading partners. Our people don't leave our village. We are not a threat to you."

"Do you not understand? You are a threat for existing." He smirked. "Now, I will have you, and your cedars, and your precious dragon, before long. You have nothing to offer me. I just wanted to understand how pathetic you really were." His eyes turned to the soldier gripping me tightly. "Get her out of my sight."

I wouldn't go gently. Even if I had no power to stop them, I would not allow them to take me without a fight. I kicked and screamed and wriggled as much as I could while the soldier pulled me from the tent. As the midday sun hit my face, a large shadow covered it for a moment, and in the darkness, I saw salvation in the form of a great dragon.

Ewig had come, and Renata rode on his back. Stupid girl. I promised her to secrecy, but in that moment, I was as glad to see her as I had ever been to see anyone.

"Well," Lord Bessinger growled, exiting the tent as his eyes tilted skyward. "This just became interesting."

Chapter 41

My immediate excitement at seeing Renata and Ewig was quickly replaced with fear when I realized Ewig was flying into a platoon of soldiers hellbent on taking him down, and Renata hadn't fought anything bigger than Leyhan since I had known her.

There was still time to end this if they simply flew away, but I knew better than that.

"This is too perfect," Lord Bessinger said with a grin. "We barely had to use you as bait for him to come calling."

"Lord Bessinger!" Ewig boomed. "You will release my property and her paramour right now, or you will see the full power of a dragon scorned and irate."

Lord Bessinger covered his eyes as he looked up into the sky. "I'm afraid we don't negotiate with terrorists, even if they are dragon lords. You are welcome to land, and we can discuss this like civilized folk."

"I have never known you to be civilized, *Armand.*" Ewig growled, really hitting the name with as much contempt as he could. "Cruel, vindictive, and stubborn, yes, but civilized...no, a fancy suit of golden armor can't mask the stink of barbarism that wafts off you."

"I remember how much you enjoyed my family's barbarism when we fought side by side in the Godwars. Now, you look down on it, but I know what you did, and how you reveled in the gore of battle."

"Enough!" Renata screamed, pointing her bow down at us. "Let Gilda go this instant!"

"No, I don't think I will." In a single, fluid motion, Lord Bessinger reached for his belt and pulled a dagger from its sheath, before sliding it an inch from my neck. "Do you think you can fire that bow before I cut your friend down?"

"If you kill her, I will burn this camp to the ground," Ewig growled.

"There's the barbarism I have always known you to possess. Kill all these men because I dared to slaughter one little girl. Who is the savage now, dragon?"

"You have five seconds," Renata growled.

"Then it seems as though we are at an impasse." Lord Bessinger nicked me lightly with his dagger, just enough to draw a few drops of crimson blood. "I think I'm being reasonable. Stow your bow and land, and I will put away my dagger, and we can discuss this like the gentlemen we both pretend to be."

Ewig flapped his wings fast enough to cause a windstorm, as dust kicked everywhere, but Lord Bessinger didn't move. If anything, he was more resolute and stoic. After a long moment, the wind subsided, and the great dragon hovered in the air.

"Fine," he said. "Renata, stow your bow."

"But—"

"No buts," Ewig growled. "Stow it."

Renata waited for Lord Bessinger to move his knife away from my neck before she lowered her bow, and Ewig settled on the ground with a great thud that shook the ground under us.

"That's better." A menacing grin rose on Lord Bessinger's face as he slid his dagger back into its sheath.

"Do not move against me, or I will be forced to burn this whole camp to the ground."

"Oh, I am very aware of your power, Ewig. Your sister speaks of it often with great reverence. Did you know that of all her brothers and sisters, you are the one she frets about the most?"

"And why is that?" Ewig growled.

"Because you cannot be appeased by gold, or knowledge, or power. It is easy to keep the others under her thumb, but you, you seem motivated by something else."

"The desire to be left alone."

Lord Bessinger chuckled. "Funny, considering for the past hundred years you have harbored fugitives within your midst. It would have been so much quieter if you simply killed them."

"I gave up that life," Ewig said.

"And yet you are willing to slaughter this whole battalion. The old Ewig must be very close to the surface. Tell me, is it tiring to keep it tamped down? Wouldn't it be easier if you just let it out to play?" His eyes were wide with fury and excitement. "I would very much like to see that."

"No, you would not," Ewig said. "Now, tell me what you want?"

"I already told you. Your sister demands all of the cedars, their families, and you, to be imprisoned, lest we raze the whole of Yesiburgh to the ground." Lord Bessinger stepped forward. "Of course, you already made your choice. We saw you evacuate your precious cedars earlier this morning."

"You cannot have them," Ewig said. "But you can have me. In exchange for their lives, and the lives of the town, I will go with you peacefully, and without incident."

"NO!" I shouted. "You can't!"

"Yes, I can!" he shouted. "And how dare you offer to give yourself up to protect me? You are mine to command, and I will not be undermined!"

"Renata!" I shouted. "You told. You promised!"

"I'm sorry, but I did," she said. "Besides, he already mostly figured it out. I just filled in the hazy bits."

"You had no right!" Ewig said.

"I speak for you," I replied. "That is what you said when I took the post on the city council, and I did what I thought you would want."

"Lies!" he growled. "I have done everything I can to keep you safe, and you walk into the lion's den."

"I found the Black Charter," I said, nearly out of breath. "I know you changed it."

"Yes, old boy," Lord Bessinger said. "Quite a nice bit of trickery there. How did you manage it?"

"Please," Ewig said. "Dragon paper was my family's specialty for generations, and human handwriting is easy enough to forge, especially when only one word needs to be changed. This was not on them. It was on me. They are innocents."

"Nobody is innocent here," he said. "But you make an interesting proposition. I was willing to lose a hundred, two hundred men fighting you to exhaustion with the hope of bringing you in alive. If I can save their lives, then perhaps, yes, that would be worth a trade, I think."

"I thought you didn't care about your men?" I said.

"Every battle is a calculation. It was not worth it to exchange you for the other cedars, but the dragon is another matter. My men might be pawns, but I prefer to keep them on the board as long as possible."

"What say you?" Ewig asked. "The town, and the cedars, for me. That is the deal I make with you."

He shook his head, pointing at me and Renata in turn. "All of the cedars, save for these two, and the boy."

"No deal," Ewig grumbled.

Lord Bessinger pointed to me. "This one is your voice on the council." Then, he pointed at Renata. "And that one killed one of the emperor's citizens. They are totems, tokens, that represent the whole, and the boy represents what happens when you ally yourself with rebels."

"No!" I screamed. "You have to let Leyhan go!"

"Gilda!" Renata screamed. "Be reasonable. We can save the whole town, and all of our sisters, in exchange for four lives. It's more than worth it." She slid down from Ewig's back and held out her hand. "I accept."

Ewig growled for a long moment. "They will not be hurt?"

"You have my word. They will be treated like princesses. On my honor."

"You have no honor," Ewig said.

"On my dishonor then."

Ewig, after a long moment, laid his head on the ground. "Then, I accept as well."

Chapter 42

They threw Renata and I into a prison cart and slammed the door closed. The walls were black metal on three sides, with a wrought-iron door the only portal that looked out into the world. It pointed front, toward a pair of white horses, or they were once white, but time has grayed them with the dust and muck of traveling the countryside.

A small man in a wool cap with flaps on either side hopped onto the cart and waved at us. His white arms were rail-thin and his clothes hung loose on his body.

"Afternoon, ladies. I'll be your driver. Don't bother learning my name, because I sure as shooting won't learn yours. It's gonna be a bumpy ride to the capitol, I'm afraid, and they spared every expense to make this cabin the least comfortable in all the kingdom."

"Why are you telling us all of this?" I asked.

"Because you have the right to know, don't you? Knowledge is the only thing the capitol can't take away from us." He smiled, showing the massive gaps in his teeth, and how they overlapped with each other. Several pointed in the wrong direction and others were nearly perpendicular to his gum. "Now, we'll be getting along any time now. Just waiting for one more."

Leyhan. He was talking about Leyhan but didn't say my love's name. Instead, he muttered something about checking the axles, and hopped down. I was mercifully happy he was gone, but then I only had Renata for company, and I was even less interested in talking to her than our overeager driver.

"I'm not sorry," Renata said. "I want you to know that."

"You have never been sorry for anything. Why would I expect anything different from you about betraying my trust?" I said. "What about my mother? She didn't go with the first group, and she didn't come with you. Where did she go?"

"When she found out what you were going to do—she didn't take it well, and we didn't have time to stop, so we left her in the caves with Mari."

"You told her!" I shouted. I tried to lunge at her, but my shackles kept me bound to my seat. "How could you?"

"She deserved to know, and you didn't tell her." Her eyes dropped. "I thought you told her. When I found out you didn't, it was too late. Why didn't you tell her?"

"I wanted her to have the memory that I might return. The last time I sacrificed myself for the greater good, she didn't have that."

"That's the dumbest thing I ever heard," Renata replied.

"Dumber than riding on a dragon to my rescue?" My eyes found hers. "Why did you come anyway? You could have run and made a life for yourself better than anyone."

"I thought I would be a prize for them, that maybe I would sweeten the pot. With the others, well, they didn't do anything wrong, except existing, but I killed somebody. They couldn't let me go." She smiled. "Seems I was right."

"And what about the food?" I asked. "Ewig was supposed to bring it on the second trip."

"They'll be fine, Gilda. It's the two of us you should be worried about."

But I wasn't worried about us. We were survivors, Renata and I. We would be fine, somehow. We would survive. The others, alone in the woods... How long would they wait before they realized we weren't coming?

As I wondered that, the door to the cell opened again and a dirt-faced boy dressed in rags was thrown in with us. Even caked in muck, I knew he was my poor, sweet Leyhan.

"My love!" I shouted, leaning forward to try and grab him in my arms. When that didn't work, I nuzzled my head on his. "I missed you so much."

His face met mine, and the devastation the soldiers had wrought on it came into stark focus. His left eye was swollen shut, and his nose was three sizes bigger than I remembered. When he smiled at me, his two front teeth had been ripped from the top of his jaw, and his right cheek was swollen.

"Sit down, meat!" a soldier shouted, tossing him into the seat next to me. They shackled him into the cart and slammed the door closed behind them when they were done.

Leyhan couldn't keep his head up, so he crashed onto my shoulder with a deep sigh. "Why did you … come—"

"I couldn't leave you," I said. "Not when—my lords, I couldn't even imagine what they would do to you."

"And I'm here because I'm an idiot," Renata said.

"That tracks." Leyhan tried to chuckle, but it came out as a wince. "You should have stayed away."

"We couldn't," I said. "They were going to hurt the cedars and raze the town if we didn't do anything. We saved everyone else, at the cost of ourselves."

"It was a small price to pay, really," Renata said. "After all, we're supposed to be dead anyway."

The cart squeaked and jostled as the driver hopped back onto it. "Alright! Everybody's here. Now, we're gonna just keep going until nightfall, so I hope you don't get motion sick." He shook his head. "Who am I kidding? I don't care either way. If you have to vomit, there's a little vent on the ground in the back. Try to aim there."

With that he scrambled to the top of the cart and snapped a whip at the horses. They whinnied and kicked as they started to ride. This was the furthest I had ever been from my home, and I would never see it again.

Chapter 43

The woods were thick with trees, so it was hard to tell when night fell until we finally stopped for the night. The driver didn't offer us water or food. He simply hopped down and walked off. I slept uneasily, laying my head on Leyhan's as he laid his on my shoulder. Even though we were in the most horrible situation I could imagine, I would rather go through it with Leyhan than lead a quiet, comfortable life without him.

"Are we there yet?" Leyhan asked as he wiped the drool from his mouth.

"I don't think so. We aren't even through the woods on the eastern panhandle yet. We have days to go before we reach the capitol."

"Days?" Renata said, stretching as best she could having been shackled to the metal bench under her. "Can they please just kill me now? I have never been in such pain before."

"Me either," Leyhan said.

Renata took one look at his mashed face and grimaced. "Right, sorry. You win. You look horrible."

"At least I feel horrible, too," he said, trying to smile but failing miserably. "Maybe it would have been better if you just killed me that night."

"Leyhan!" I shouted. "Don't even joke about that."

"What?" Renata replied. "You've never thought about how much easier it would be if Ewig had not been a coward and eaten you?"

"No! Never."

"You are such a liar, and a bad one, too." Renata shook her hair free of her face. "It's okay. You're not a bad person for thinking death would be the easy way out. Existence is the pits."

"Well, I quite like it," I said, lying through my teeth, but unwilling to give Renata the satisfaction of the truth. "Even in the worst of times."

"You really are awful. I thought your inane optimism was bad before when I could walk away from it, but it's torture now. Maybe if I scream loud enough, the guards will come and beat my head in."

"I wouldn't do that if I were you," a voice harshly whispered from the side of the van. When they leapt up onto the cab, it was a person I hadn't seen before, nearly feral, with dark brown clothes and darker hair that covered every inch of him. "Alert the guards and I can't get you out."

"Who are y—"

"Shhhh," he said. "I've gone to quite a bit of trouble to get this, and we don't have much time." He raised a key from his hand and stuck it into the door. When it turned, my heart leapt into my throat. "Can you all walk?"

"First tell me who you are—" The man glared at me with deep green eyes that said we didn't have time for questions. "Yes, I can."

He turned to Leyhan. "And what about you, son? They got you good. Are your legs broken?"

Leyhan shook his head as the man unlocked his chains. "No, sir. I can walk."

"Excellent." He moved to me. "When I tell you, move out of the cabin and hop down into the woods on your left. Keep low."

"Thank you," I said, rubbing my free hands. "But we are supposed to be captors of the empire in exchange for the freedom of our village. We can't go with you."

"That's dumb," the man said. "Lord Bessinger has lied to you, and if you come with me, I'll tell you how, but we have to go now."

"Well, that's good enough for me. I'm going," Renata said. "I've been a prisoner for most of the day and I don't like it at all. Thank you, sir."

"Don't thank me yet," he replied, turning to Renata. "If they catch us, they'll roast us on a spit for desertion. You can thank me when we're free from this place." He finished opening Renata's cuffs. "Okay, now—go."

Leyhan led the way out of the cab, jumping down into the brush next to it. Renata followed, and I took up the back, followed only by the feral man. When I hopped down into the woods, I saw the outline of a man, bleeding from the head. I looked back to see the feral man's hands covered in blood.

"I'm not sure about this," I said to him. "We really—"

He pushed me forward. "I know you don't trust me, but I swear on my life I would not save you without a reason. I have lived in these woods a long time, and I would not make myself known unless it was important."

His voice had certainty and gravitas to it, which gave me confidence to follow him. "Okay."

"Don't stop," the feral man said, pushing us forward.

"Now that we're free, who are you?" I asked pointedly.

"Is that really important right now?"

"What if you are worse than the guards? What if you are going to torture us alive? Yes, of course it's important. But most importantly, why don't you want to tell us?"

"I'm not going to torture you, and as for why I'm trying so hard to avoid the topic...I've been waiting to meet you for a long time, and I certainly didn't think this was how I would meet my little girl again."

I stopped in my tracks and turned to him. He smiled through his bushy beard. It was an awkward smile, and his eyes cried out in fear.

"Dad?" I said.

"Hi, kiddo. Sorry it's been so long."

Chapter 44

My father. The one who disappeared when I was a child to live in the woods after being exiled from Yesiburgh, had just saved my life, and now stared awkwardly at me, his daughter, in the middle of the woods.

"What do you mean?" I said. "You're my father?"

"Can we explain while we move?" He looked over my shoulder. "They are going to notice that poor chap is dead sooner than later, and we need to be far away when they do." He looked past me to Renata. "Nice to see you again, by the way."

"It's hard to believe it's you," Renata said. "I remember the day you left."

"Yes, yes. I know this is a lot to process. Seriously, though. Let's move, or this reunion will be short lived and bittersweet."

He pushed us forward, and I begrudgingly started to move through the brush. My father moved from the back of us to the front to lead our little pack, and we picked up speed as we moved through the brambles, into little pockets and holes in the brush that only he seemed to see.

"Have you been living in the woods this whole time?" I asked.

"Not quite the whole time, but enough of it to know my way around." He looked back at me as he continued forward, as if he had every confidence in his ability to move through the dark. "I lived in Janiston for a while, but everything reminded me of you there."

"If you were alive, why didn't you come back for me?"

"I wanted to, kiddo, I really did, but I knew Renata would take care of you."

"Excuse me?" Renata said. "How did you know—"

"That Ewig didn't kill his sacrifices? Oh, some years into my wandering I made my way into the forbidden woods, and that's where I saw Fadia and Freja toiling away."

"Why didn't you say anything?" Leyhan asked.

"Are you kidding? Who would I tell that wouldn't want to immediately try to kill them for their insolence?"

"Yes, Leyhan," Renata said in agreement. "Weird how that happens."

Dad shook his head. "No, I knew that the best way to find you would be to wait until you were 'sacrificed' and then come for you. Of course, by the time I came for you, the whole thing had imploded, and you moved back to town." He turned left through a little hole in the bushes. "I really was planning on coming for you, kiddo, but, well, look at me, and then with your mother...it's just a lot, and I didn't want to rush it. Of course, the universe conspired to force the situation."

"How did you find us?" Renata asked.

"It wasn't hard. The royal army doesn't travel in secret. When they showed up, I knew what they wanted. I had to bide my time. I was just lucky it was only a small contingent that left to bring you to prison. If I had to fight off many more soldiers, I don't think I would have been able to rescue you."

"I—I—I can't believe this," I said, shaking my head.

Renata laughed. "Really? After all the craziness we've been through for the last year, this is the thing that pushes it over the edge?"

"Well, it has to be something doesn't it? And yeah, this is just one too many crazy things to happen all at once."

Dad turned around and placed his hands in mine. "I know this is hard, and I wish it was going to get easier, but I need your help to save Ewig. Otherwise, who knows what will happen to him, and the town."

My face turned hard. "What's wrong with the town?"

"Before I left after you, I heard them say they were going to burn the town to ash."

"Those—" I growled. "They promised. That was part of the deal."

"Oh, yeah, leave it to dishonorable men not to keep their word," Renata said. "Frankly, I say let them burn."

"No!" I shouted. "We can't let them die. And now, if you remember, my mother is there, along with Mari, so even if you don't want to save anyone else, you left my mother there to die, too."

Renata growled at me. "Fine, you're right. Alright. So, we have to free Ewig, and then save the day. What is your plan?"

Dad smirked. "I figured we would just wing it."

"Oh great," Leyhan said. "That's just perfect."

"Kidding," Dad said, missing the ironic tone of his voice. "I have it all worked out. Now, come on. We're only going to have one chance at this."

Chapter 45

We moved backwards for hours, moving closer and closer to town, zig-zagging through the trees and taking advantage of every break in the forest. Finally, with the sun breaking through the sky again, we stopped at a gap in the road where the road narrowed.

"Help me with this," Dad said, grabbing the edge of a rotten tree.

We all leaned into the edge of it, and with a snap it came tumbling down across the path. Then, he pulled a spool of rope from the brush and rushed a hundred feet from the brand. The rest of us caught up to him as he tied it around a hearty tree. He handed the thread to Renata.

"Bring this across the road. Cover it in the dirt, but don't pull it taut. Understood?"

"Yes, sir," she replied, leaping into the road. "Consider it done."

"Are you a strong climber?" Dad asked Leyhan.

"Not with the beating I took," he replied.

"That's okay, boy. Then you will be the lookout. Can you whistle?"

He nodded. "Like a nightingale."

"Good, good. Then when you see Ewig's caravan, whistle out just like a nightingale. They should be along any time now."

"Are you sure?" I asked.

"They were not far behind you on the road when I last checked, and I overheard they were going to ride through the night to catch up to your caravan. They were eager to get the dragon lord back to the capitol." He looked across the road as Renata gave a thumbs up to him. "They are a small group now, but when they connect with the others, they will be unstoppable. This is our only chance."

I nodded. "Then what can I do?"

"This is all going to happen quickly." He pulled a vial of black sand out of his pocket. "This is a new weapon they are developing in the capitol. It has the power of a dragon but can fit in a weapon soldiers can hold in their hand."

"That little thing?" I said. "It doesn't look like much."

"That's the beauty of it. I stole some off the cab of an alchemist's truck two years ago, knowing it would be of use." He pointed to the top of the tree. "I will set it with a wick once I climb this tree. When it explodes, I need you to run up to Ewig's carrier, and set him free."

"He thinks he's saving everyone. We all thought we were saving everyone."

"Which is why I need you to tell him the truth. He will not believe me, but he will believe you." He must have seen my hesitation. "You do believe me, don't you?"

"I—" I looked him deep in his green eyes. "I want to, but you're like a stranger to me."

He bit his lip, trying to prevent himself from crying. While he formulated the words, he heard a nightingale coo. "That must be your friend." He reached into his coat and pulled a large key from it. "I will earn your trust in time, but I need you to take it on faith that I want nothing but the best for you."

I nodded, gripping the heavy, black key in my hand. "Okay."

He turned to the tree, then looked at me from over his shoulder. "If you fail, they will capture us, and not hesitate to kill us. The only thing that can prevent our death is Ewig's freedom."

"No pressure." I let out a deep sigh. "No problem. I have this."

"That's my girl," he said with a smile as he climbed the tree.

I watched him disappear into the canopy before my eyes turned to the rumble on the road. Two horses led a massive wooden cart, with Ewig shackled down on top of it by the neck, and all four of his legs. On either side of him three soldiers rode on horseback, carrying lances, and another two pulled up the rear. They weren't much protection, given the cargo, but if they were allowed to meet up with the others, and they were joined with even more of the army, then my father was right, it would be impossible to stop them again.

"Whoa." One of the riders held up their hand, as the others stopped. "Branch on the road. Be on the lookout for traps, men."

The two men in the front rode forward with another side from either side of the cart, leaving two on either side, and two behind. I moved forward, passing the soldiers as I went. When I was perpendicular to the cart, I crouched low, ready to bolt forward at a moment's notice.

"NOW!" my dad shouted, and Renata's rope rose, tripping two of the horses. My dad leapt from the tree throwing the black powder in front of him. When it hit the ground, the powder exploded, sending other horses rearing into the air.

In the chaos I rushed forward and pulled myself onto the cart. "Ewig! You're okay."

"Gilda? What are you doing here? You're supposed to be captured."

"It's a long story, but Lord Bessinger lied to us. Yesiburgh is in trouble. They are razing it right now."

"Who told you such nonsense?" Ewig growled.

"I did," my father said. "Hi, I'm her dad. I can tell you it's not nonsense. I only wish it was."

"Hey!" the guards shouted. They were beginning to recover. "Get down from there!"

"We don't have time, dragon lord," my dad said. "We need you to get you free and to safety. You are the town's only help."

"And I'm supposed to take advice from somebody who abandoned his daughter?"

"No," I replied. "You're supposed to trust me, and I believe him. It's the exact kind of thing

Lord Bessinger would do. Wait until they're helpless, and then slaughter them."

"I must admit, that is like him." Ewig thought for a short moment. "Very well. Free me!"

I unlocked his neck first. As I went for his leg, a lance swiped at me. I leapt over it and unlocked his front left foot. When it came free, the giant talon knocked both the soldiers off their mounts. I made my way to the back leg, and when I had it free, Ewig kicked the soldiers in the back off their horses. By the time I made it to his right legs, the great dragon lord had already swiped his neck and knocked the final soldiers off their steers.

"You had better be right about this," Ewig said. "Or we just condemned your whole town to death for defying my sister."

In the distance, I saw the other soldiers, the ones who were protecting my cart, rush forward from a distance. They must have followed us back. Meanwhile, the other soldiers were beginning to right themselves and ready for a fight.

I leapt onto Ewig's back. "We don't have time to think about it too much." I grabbed my father's hand and pulled him up, and Renata made it up by herself. Leyhan was last, hampered by his beating, but he made it up as well, finally, and we lifted into the air.

"I do so hate being a beast of burden."

"Then just think of yourself as a hero, saving all four of us at once."

"Hrm," Ewig said, rising higher in the air as lances and arrows flew harmlessly around him. Those that hit his skin bounced off as if it was nothing. "I do like that. 'Dragon Lord Ewig, hero of Yesiburgh' has a nice ring to it."

Chapter 46

When we broke the tree line, I saw the smoke rising high into the air and knew my father was telling the truth. A big part of me hoped he was manipulating me, even as I was following his orders, but once I saw the fires for myself, it was impossible to deny he was right.

"My gods," Ewig growled. "And they call me a monster."

"Less talking and more flying!" Renata shouted.

"Hang on tight!" Ewig shouted. "I've never gone this fast with people on my back before."

The wind hit my face painfully and forcefully as we sped through the air. I leaned forward and hugged Ewig's back, careful to create a pocket for myself to trap air so that I could breathe even as he cut through the sky, rising higher and higher with each passing second.

The cloud cover helped protect us from Lord Bessinger's attack, but it also prevented me from seeing the position of the troops from the air. The only landmark that jutted above the clouds was the volcano, and with every flap of his powerful wings, we flew closer and closer to it.

When the volcano dominated my view, Ewig dove below the clouds, and I saw that most of the army had vacated the clearing they once occupied, where Lord Bessinger had lied directly to my face.

As we fell toward the ground, Ewig opened his mouth and fire erupted from it, bathing the whole of the encampment in a blazing inferno that sent everything up in flames from the tents to the weapons to the men.

"Let's not make the fires any bigger, yes?" I whispered into his ear.

"I am a dragon with few talents save burninating the countryside."

He made two more passes through the camp and by the time he was done, there was not an ounce of the camp that was not in flames. He watched it burn, the cries of the soldiers, and the crackle of the flames, before he hovered in the air and flapped his majestic wings fast enough to send a powerful gust of wind through the campsite, dousing all the flames before they could spread to the forest, and leaving nothing but the charred remains of the army behind.

When he was done, Ewig darted through the air and reached the town, the same one it took me hours to walk from, in under a minute. I nearly fell from his back with the force of his movements, but I managed to keep my bearings as the great dragon lord shot through the sky.

He landed with a giant thud as he reached the edge of town. In front of us, the fire burned brightly. "You don't want to see this part. Stay back."

The four of us slid off his back and he rose back into the air with a loud screech.

"We're not going to listen to him, right?" Renata said from being me.

"Of course not," I replied. "We haven't for as long as I've known him. Why start now?"

As he flew above, I rushed into the town to see the stores and shops on fire, down to the last one. We reached the square quickly, to see everything from the school to the city hall to the church glowing orange and crackling in the fire.

All around us soldiers fought with townspeople. Some had weapons, but the majority of Yesiburgh was defenseless. Even those with a sword barely knew how to use it, and the ground was littered with the bodies of the dead.

"What are we supposed to do?" Renata shouted. Her yells caught the attention of a soldier, but by the time they turned to attack, Renata shot two arrows into their chest.

"That's a good start," Leyhan said.

My father knelt and picked a sword from a desecrated heap of a man. When a pair of soldiers attacked him with pikes, he gracefully slid between them, and then slid his sword through their bodies.

Meanwhile, the shrieks from Ewig filled the air as the soldiers turned through focus on the great dragon. It was no contest, though, as Ewig was impervious to their attacks. He picked them off one, two, or sometimes six at a time, until there were none left in the square, and the soldier bodies piled as high as the townspeople.

"Bernice!" I shouted, recognizing one of the bloodied bodies. I rushed to her and slid down, grabbing her bloody hand with mine. "No, no, no, no, no."

Her eyes went wide. "You came back. He came to save us. I knew it."

"Just stay still, okay. We'll get a doctor and…"

But it was no use. I watched her convulse, give one last heave of her breasts, and then fall over, dead, her lifeless eyes staring back up at me.

"*NOOOO!*" I shouted, pounding my fists on the ground.

Great gusts of wind flew through the square as Ewig worked to single handedly try to douse the flames. Then, a horrifying thought shot through my mind, which stood out in a sea of horrible images.

Mom. I needed to get to her. I took off bolting through the square. I was not much of a runner, but I had built up some stamina during the year since my cedar.

I was halfway across the square when a soldier took notice of me and rushed forward. I realized then I could not protect myself. I could not defend myself. He swung his mace to attack, and I braced myself for the hit, but the hit never came. Instead, an arrow shot through the man's head, and he fell down dead.

"Where are you going?" Renata asked, still holding her bow at attention.

"I have to find my mom."

"Then we're going with you." Leyhan reached down and pulled the mace from the man's hand as my father readied himself to follow me. "We have to stick together. Got it?"

I nodded. "Got it."

Chapter 47

We fought our way across town until we reached the bridge to Ewig's cave. Saying that we fought is a bit of a misnomer, though, because I had little to do with the fight, except to scream and yelp when another soldier turned their attention to us. I had managed to grab a sword from a dead soldier, but it was heavy even with two hands.

Two arrows whizzed by my head, and I saw an archer in the distance. Renata took aim and dropped the archer with three arrows, two of which flew wide, but the final one hit them right in the throat.

The path to Ewig's keep was difficult to traverse in a hurry, and I found myself breathing deeply and taking each step slowly lest I rush forward and slide to my death. I wondered for a moment how many soldiers fell on their way across the chasm, and it made me smile to hope it was many of them.

It was a horrible thought, and I hated that my mind went there, but whatever did this to my people was not human. It had no empathy, and it justified every bit of Gertrude's fear. Though they were wrong to blame us for this attack, especially since we had given ourselves up to avoid it, they were right to fear the army, and its brutality.

When I reached the entrance to the cave, I heard guttural growls and frightened screams echoing from within. My mother did not have much occasion to scream, but I still recognized her voice on the air.

"Mom!" I screamed as I took off like a bolt through the cave. "Mari!"

Heavy footsteps lined the cave as I made it through to Ewig's keep. The fire had been knocked over, and several gems had been pulled from the walls, and now rested on the floor.

"You must be the cedars." Two soldiers turned to us, rising from their packs. "Perfect timing."

They attacked, and my father rushed past me to defend, slicing one in half while Leyhan slammed his mace into the other's skull. They dropped to the ground.

I didn't stop to wait for them, bolting through the tunnel toward the dining area, where the screams were growing louder. When I broke through to the other side, I saw that the rope bridge had been sliced, and barely hung, and only then because we re-enforced in the last year. Beyond it, my mother swung a cast-iron pan at two more soldiers. Mari stood behind her with a cleaver, swiping it wildly at the attacking soldiers.

I couldn't wait. I hopped onto what was left of the bridge and shimmied across it carefully, my heart stopping every time it jerked one way or another. I never liked the rope bridge, but half of it falling way made it lose its sense of stability, and now I hated it even more.

"Wait for us!" Renata screamed at me. "You can't even fight!"

I didn't answer. I was too concerned with keeping my balance on the bridge, which grew harder still when Renata responded to my silence by joining me on the bridge, and Leyhan after her, followed in the rear by my father.

The bridge might have been swaying heavily, but it held firm as ever to its pitons and I made it across without overwhelming effort. I gripped the sword tightly in my hands and leapt down the stairs.

"Get your hands off them!" I screamed.

The two soldiers turned to me with a smile, each brandishing a war hammer in their hands. One of them rushed me first, swinging the hammer. I ducked to avoid it and swung my sword. The sword connected with the soldier's shin, and he yelped in pain.

"You little bi—I'm going to kill you!"

He turned to attack, when an arrow flew through his eye, dropping him instantly. Renata turned to the last soldier. "Step away!"

"You really think you have the accuracy to hit me with one shot?" The soldier said. "Cuz you got as good a shot at hitting them as me, way I see it."

"Shoot him!" Mari screamed.

"Don't bother!" my dad shouted, leaping down next to me. "Get away from my wife, right now."

"Horace?" my mother asked.

"Good to see you, Odine. Wish it was under better circumstances."

The soldier went for my mother with the hammer, and she blocked it with her pan. This attack angered my father, who rushed forward and sliced the soldier across the back. The man winced in pain, and my dad took his shuddering as an opportunity to skewer him through the side with another blow.

When the soldier fell, my mother smiled at my dad. Without a word, she leapt into his arms, and they kissed like they had never left each other. It was a touching moment in the carnage of the day; the cherry on top of a very horrible sundae.

"Don't you ever leave me again, okay?" my mother said, breaking from him.

"You know I can't promise that, love. After all, somebody's gotta clean all this mess up." He turned to me. "And I have a feeling our daughter's going to have a part in that."

Chapter 48

Renata shimmied back across the rope bridge and helped me secure it back to its posts, and we made our way back out to the front of the cavern. By the time we arrived, Ewig finished putting out the fires, and landed in the middle of the square to take on the last of Lord Bessinger's troops.

"Remind me never to piss him off," Renata said. "That dragon is unstoppable."

It was true. He defeated dozens, hundreds of troops without a second thought, and without taking much time, either. I couldn't imagine what they could do on a battlefield, and understood why 11 dragons could run the world, and drive back the gods.

"Come on," I said, climbing down the cliff. "Let's go help."

"I don't think we're going to be doing much help," Leyhan replied. "I think he's doing just fine on his own."

"I'll stay here and look after him," Mari said.

"Suit yourself." I kept climbing. "I'm going, though."

"You're going to get yourself killed one of these days," Renata said, joining me in my descent.

"I should already be dead, so that doesn't scare me."

I continued down the path to the town, where Ewig's roars grew louder, and his movements made the ground shake. When he saw me, he finished batting around the soldier in his grasp and tossed him a hundred feet across the square, into the smoldering ruins of Nur's bakery.

"Hello, little pet. So nice of you to join me."

"Sorry to spoil your fun," I said. "But you saved the whole city. You're a hero."

"What little there is left to save," he replied. "There are still soldiers cowering in homes, along the side streets, but I am hoping we can gather whoever is left and ferret them out."

"I'm sure we can make that happen," Renata said, rubbing her neck. "Are you sure there's anyone left?"

"Oh sure," Ewig replied. "I've seen them from the corner of my eyes as I fought and saved a few from attacks. The emperor's army tried their hardest, but they couldn't wipe this place off the face of the map." He turned to me. "They will try, though, again, if we do not show there is fight in us to protect what is ours."

I nodded. "Then we will fight."

"Yes, we will," Ewig said. "That is a battle for another day, though. Right now, we need to bury our dead, and gather the living."

"The caves are the only place not burnt to a crisp," Renata said.

"Then that is where we will gather them," Ewig said. "Tell everyone left breathing that I will protect them, personally, if they join us in the caves."

"They wouldn't do this for you, you know," Renata said. "For any of us."

"Some of them would," I replied, thinking of Bernice. "And even if they wouldn't, that's not what's important. What they put in the world is their problem, but what we put is ours, and I will put out love for as long as I can."

"What about when you attacked that soldier? Was that love?"

"In a way; love for my mother, and for Mari." I caught her eyes. "Just because I preach love and tolerance doesn't mean I won't fight for mine."

"When they find out that we have survived, they will come with everything they have. They do not want a hint of rebellion to be left standing. If it is, then hope will grow in it. Right now, we are that hope for everyone that has ever wanted freedom from my sister. They will do everything they can to stamp our embers out."

"They can try."

They did try to snuff us out, to destroy us, but we survived, and we will rebuild. We will rise from the ashes like a phoenix and burn this whole system to the ground.

Count on it.

Author's Note

The goal for this series was simple. Can I make a book interesting without having the world end on every page? It has been an incredibly hard challenge. For me, writing small moments is WAY harder than world ending ones. After all, when you have world changing moments, the tension is already ratcheted up just by the simple fact of the world literally ending.

In this book, it takes nearly 20% of the book for them to make it to dinner, and a good 25% before the main action is set in motion. This is, in comics at least, called decompressed storytelling, and I have been against it for a long time. However, recently I've worked with some artists: Angela Oddling, Claire Donaghue, and Cammry Lapka among them, who helped me see the great joy of spending a whole page or two watching somebody eat a sandwich or walk across the street.

Claire was the original artist of the graphic novel, back when this was a graphic novel. When I wrote the original graphic novel script, I was very conscious to make sure not much happened while at the same time, entire universes turned on the edge of these small moments.

It wasn't until I got a little older, a little wiser, and a little more patient that I could appreciate luxuriating in these small moments, and really falling in love with them. This kind of storytelling draws focus to one moment in time and gives more context to the big moments that make up the climaxes of most books.

I don't think I'll ever write a book series this slow paced again, but I've already seen how this series has helped me write *The Obsidian Spindle Saga* and take more time with the character moments that exist in the white space between the big bits of action.

I think I even went further with the "beauty in the small moments" parts of this book than I did with the previous installment, with the pace of action really only picking up after Gilda and the group were freed from their cage from her father.

Speaking of, what did you think of that reveal? They say you're not supposed to set something up if you don't chop it down in the same book, but I always knew Gilda's father would make an appearance in the second book. The hardest part was finding a place for him to pop up, especially with the pace at which everything was moving.

I'm hoping to spend more time with him in the finale, but we have to try and dismantle a whole system of government, and build a new one, and I don't have that long to do it.

I have a feeling that the luxury of these first two books is going to go away in the finale, *The Dragon Goddess,* but I have to make sure not to make it move too fast, because I still want to find these little moments to enjoy throughout. If you read my note in the previous installment, then you know that I've had this queued up for years now, and the idea has been sitting with me for even longer. Though this is a huge departure for me, and something I probably won't ever do again, I'm so proud of how this story is turning out, and what Gilda has grown into, and will hopefully keep growing into during the next book as well.

I hope you are super excited for the finale of this trilogy, *The Dragon Goddess.* I know I am.

Also by Russell Nohelty

THE OBSIDIAN SPINDLE SAGA
The Sleeping Beauty
The Wicked Witch
The Fairy Queen
The Red Rider
THE GODVERSE CHRONICLES
And Death Followed Behind Her
And Doom Followed Behind Her
And Ruin Followed Behind Her
And Hell Followed Behind Her
And Conquest Followed Behind Them
And Darkness Followed Behind Her
And Chaos Followed Behind Them
Katrina Hates the Dead
Pixie Dust

OTHER NOVEL WORK
My Father Didn't Kill Himself
Sorry for Existing
Gumshoes: The Case of Madison's Father
The Invasion Saga
The Vessel
Worst Thing in the Universe
The Void Calls Us Home
The Marked Ones

OTHER ILLUSTRATED WORK
The Little Bird and the Little Worm
Ichabod Jones: Monster Hunter
Gherkin Boy
www.russellnohelty.com

www.ingramcontent.com/pod-product-compliance
Lightning Source LLC
Chambersburg PA
CBHW071143180726
48291CB00007B/2319